Very N

By Dana Marie Bell

Dana Marie Bell Books
www.danamariebell.com

Dana Marie Bell
PO Box 39
Bear, DE 19701

Very Much Alive
Copyright © 2009 by Dana Marie Bell
ISBN: 978-1985311657
Edited by Angela James
Cover by Anne Cain

First Edition electronic publication by Samhain Publishing, Ltd.: February 2009
Second Edition electronic publication by Dana Marie Bell: March 2017
First Print publication: February 2018

About the Author

Dana Marie Bell lives with her husband Dusty, their two maniacal children, an evil ice-cream stealing cat and a dog who thinks barking should become the next Olympic event. You can learn more about Dana and her addiction to series at www.danamariebell.com.

Dedication

To Mom and Dad, who aren't going to get copies of this. They aren't old enough to read it yet.

To Memom, who *will* get a copy, and knowing her, will sneak it to my mother when I'm not looking.

To Anne Cain, who, quite frankly, rocks the covers! (Book covers, you pervs! Sheesh. What the heck would I know about what she does in the privacy of her boudoir?)

And to Dusty, who was man enough to sniffle when Christian Slater whispered, "Stay," and was so touched by the movie that we had Sterling roses in our wedding. Love you, sweetheart.

Prologue

Long ago…

Baldur looked down at the broken, bleeding body of the man who'd sacrificed himself so that Baldur could live.

Baldur had been furious when Loki ambushed him, binding him and silencing him with a damned Jotun spell. He'd watched, furious, as the fiery-haired man took on Baldur's face and form and strode into the Thing, the sacred space of the gods. He hadn't realized that Loki had been intent on *saving* him.

"Leave, I beg of you, before Odin returns."

The urgency in Loki's voice and face was nearly drowned out by the pain. The Trickster God coughed, bright red blood spattering onto his already soaked clothing.

Without his help, Loki would die of his wounds, so numerous and grievous that, if he hadn't been who he was, he would have died long before. The sluggish bleeding of the wound in his chest indicated that the other god's extraordinary healing powers were working, but slowly. Oh, so slowly.

The sacrifice Loki had made was something no one, least of all Baldur, would have ever expected a man like him to make. All the disdain, the annoyance at Loki's flippancy, the anger at his seeming betrayals, evaporated under the truth of a sacrifice so great it didn't bear thinking on.

So Baldur did the only thing he could think to do: offer comfort to one who'd sacrificed more than anyone before. He leaned down, pressing a soft kiss to those bruised, bleeding lips, his allegiance solidly and forever given to the man who, days before, he would have sneered at. His heart cracked and bled as even that small gesture caused the man beneath him to hiss in pain. "Have no fear. I will take care of you. Rest now; you are safe." Thunder sounded in the distance as he blanketed the man with his own cloak. Shivering slightly in the wet spring air, he turned away from Loki. "I will go and inform your daughter of what has happened here. I will return as soon as I can."

He ignored the moaning protest of the man beneath the cloak, knowing that he was doing the right thing. With a quick backwards glance he left the hiding place Loki had created for him. The pit of his stomach told him that the choice he was making might not be the best one, but what other choice was there? He couldn't allow Loki to die!

He strode through the Thing, desperate to save the one man he'd never thought he would bother to.

Loki closed his eyes wearily as Baldur left. He lifted one hand to touch his lips, still reeling from the freely given gesture. He'd seen the look on Baldur's face and knew the grief and rage of betrayal ate at him. The fact that he'd taken the time to comfort a dying man, a man feared, loathed, and reviled throughout the world, touched him as few things could these days.

He'd also seen Baldur's determination to return to him, but he knew Baldur couldn't be found here. With a groaning sigh he lifted himself, dragging himself away before the other man returned.

It was better this way. When the Aesir and Vanir found him, inflicted on him the punishment he was sure was going to come, he didn't want Baldur to see it. He knew better than to hope the other man would come to his rescue, or try to convince the others to let him go. It never worked that way for him, and it never would, no matter how his heart ached. His own actions had seen to it, helped along by Baldur's betrayer.

He staggered out into the night, the cloak wrapped around his body, the scent of the other man soothing to him. He ignored the longing in his heart for what could never be, and braced himself for what was to come.

And in the dark of the night a secret watcher raced to correct an injustice so horrendous the heavens would one day shatter from it, knowing that it was already too late...

Chapter One

Present Day…

Kiran smiled as the soft sound of a footfall behind him alerted him to Logan's presence. After all these years together he still found himself bracing for the sight of his lover's wickedly dark face. In his mind's eye, he could see the sardonic grin that would be gracing those full lips, the amusement gleaming in those dark eyes. The setting sun would light fire to that dark hair, making Kiran's fingers itch to run through it just to feel its hidden heat. Other than the fact that he was male, and a sarcastic son of a bitch at that, he was everything Kiran had once dreamed of.

But even the thought of his lover couldn't shake the anxiety that seemed to be dogging his footsteps today. Time had taught him to trust his instincts, and his instincts were screaming at him *time to go!*

A pointed chin rested on his shoulder and strong, tanned hands went around his waist. "How did I know I'd find you out here?" Kir grinned, leaning into his lover's touch. "Can't you get enough of the ocean?"

Kir gave in to temptation and reached up, fingering the dark strands that flew in the tradewinds to mingle with his, fire to his ice. "You know how much I love the ocean, Logan."

Logan snorted. "You love *everything.*"

"Some things more than others."

He shivered hard when Logan pressed a soft kiss to the side of his neck. He felt his cock twitch in interest. If Logan was in the mood to play, he'd be more than happy to accommodate him. *After* they left.

"It's time."

The smile left his face, his hands dropping from Logan's hair to tangle with the hands at his waist. He blew out a breath, anxiety over the plan Logan had come up with churning in his gut. He didn't know why, but he had the feeling something big was going to happen, something that would change both their lives. *Maybe this time we'll get the son of a bitch. Maybe that's what's churning in my gut today. Still...* "Are you *sure* about this?"

"Positive. This time I think we can beat him."

Kiran nodded, knowing that when Logan got that tone in his voice it was almost impossible to talk him out of whatever it was he had his mind set to. Better to just go along and guard his stubborn ass whether he liked it or not. But he had a very bad feeling about the whole thing, and it was making him nervous, tangling with the anxiety to *move* beating beneath his skin. "We need to take every precaution."

"Yup."

"Dot our i's. Cross our t's."

"Of course."

"Leave no stone unturned."

"Kir?"

"Pursue every lead."

"Kir!"

"Yes?"

He felt Logan's sigh against his hair. "We have an appointment we don't want to miss, remember? Or should we just chuck it all and you can go work for Hallmark?"

He waited until he heard Logan growl.

"Hey, I'm thinking about it." When Logan chuckled he was absurdly pleased.

He yelped when Logan smacked him on the ass. "Let's go, princess, or we'll be late."

Kir rubbed his ass and turned with a frown. Logan's laughing face zoomed in close as his lover planted a quick kiss on his lips.

"Last night you were on the bottom. Doesn't that make *you* the princess?"

Logan looked over his shoulder at Kir as he led the way back to their beachfront house. "Hell, no, blondie. You're way too pretty to be anything but the princess. Besides, you're the one the evil *queen* wants dead, remember?"

Kir snickered at the thought of the dour Oliver Grimm as a "queen". He'd pay big bucks to see Daddy Dearest in drag. "What does that make you? My loyal *woods*man?"

Logan turned with a groan, walking backwards towards the house. "That one was bad, Kir. Just damn awful." He turned, reached for the front doorknob, and inserted the key into the lock.

Kir was never quite sure afterwards what alerted him, but he grabbed Logan in his arms and turned him just as the house exploded around them in a huge ball of fire. They were tossed into the air like rag-dolls, burning bits and pieces of their beach hideaway raining down on them as they landed.

"God damn it, Kir! Don't *do* that!" Logan struggled out of his arms and to his feet. He glared at him, his face smudged with dirt and smoke, bits and pieces of their house sticking to his burnt clothes. A cut on his cheek healed as Kir watched. "You could have been killed! How do you know he didn't have the place littered with mistletoe toothpicks?"

Kir got to his feet with a sigh. "You're welcome."

Logan's eyes narrowed, flames dancing in their depths, letting him know just how much he'd managed to piss him off. "Don't put yourself between me and anything, Kir. We're too close to winning to die now."

"Logan."

"Fire can't hurt me, damn it!"

Kir picked up the six-foot piece of wood that had bounced off his broad back. "But this would have."

Logan's eyes widened. "Fuck. Yeah, okay, that would have pinched a bit."

"We need to get out of here." *Always trust your instincts. Damn it, I* knew *something was off today!* Kiran looked around, knowing that their car was probably totaled along with all the rest of the possessions they'd had in their home.

"Done." Logan shifted, changing into a sleek black Corvette, a trick he'd learned from visiting a pooka several years ago.

Kiran smiled as he climbed into the "car". "Damn. I like your style."

Another one of Logan's amused snorts sounded from the speakers. "I know." He roared off into the night, eager to put distance between them and any of Grimm's nearby assassins.

If Val Grimm wanted them dead, he'd had plenty of opportunities to kill them while they chatted on the beach. *What the hell is he up to, and why didn't he just take us out?* But he knew the answer to that already. Centuries' worth of fighting with the Grimms had given it to him.

Old man Grimm wanted them dead. Val wanted to play with them first.

Logan drove like a bat out of hell towards the water, letting Kir know he was still pissed at him. But Logan had given up way too much for him already. There was no way Kir would allow him to give up his life, as well.

If that meant Kir's death, then so be it. After all, as far as most of the world was concerned, he was already dead.

***

Logan was supremely pissed. A fucking island in the middle of fucking nowhere, and Grimm had *still* managed to find them and plant that damn bomb. He was so sick and tired of running and hiding that there were times he just wanted to give up, to let Grimm have him and to hell with what would happen next.

But that would mean giving up the one thing that brought his life any joy: Kiran. Old Grimm would kill Kir without a second's hesitation. He'd already proven what he was willing to do to them, child and adopted brother notwithstanding.

He made it to the edge of the water before shifting, at speed, into a small boat, carrying Kir far away from the beings who sought their deaths. He would die a thousand times over to prevent Grimm from laying one finger on Kir's pale blond hair. He would tie himself to the earth once again before he saw Kir's eyes closed in death. He would gladly suffer the acidic poison constantly dripping, driving him insane, before he would allow Kir to suffer a moment's more pain than he already had.

He would have done the same for his children if Grimm hadn't murdered them. As it was he dared not approach his living children for fear of bringing Grimm's wrath down on their heads even more.

Mentally he tried to shake off the rage still consuming him, but it wasn't easy. Kir's hand caressing the steering wheel helped. His lover knew him so well, knowing instinctively what to do to ease him.

All of it, the deaths of Kir's wife, Logan's children, the failure of his marriage and his status as a fugitive could all be laid at one manipulative bastard's door: Oliver Grimm.

And this time, the son of a bitch was going to pay for what he'd done.

***

Val Grimm walked into his father's high rise office with no expression on his face. He knew better than to show his father any sign of weakness. "They're in the city, sir."

Oliver Grimm looked at his youngest child out of chilly blue eyes. "I want them dead this time. No mistakes, Val."

"Yes, sir." Val took a breath, not happy to deliver the next bit of news to his father. "I believe they intend to contact—"

"I don't give a fuck who they contact. Get them out of my hair once and for all, understand?"

Val nodded his acquiescence, ignoring the unspoken threat. When his father got that dead tone in his voice, he knew better than to argue. Grimm had no further desire to hear anything from his failure of a youngest son until the deed had been done. He left, brows furrowed, the pounding headache lurking behind his eyes telling him exactly how shitty this day was going to be. But at least all of the players were in place, finally.

Maneuvering things so that all of them were together at the same time in the same city was a bitch and a half. Half the time they weren't paying attention, and the other half? They were off chasing their dicks. But now, all but one player was on the field, and he would be arriving soon, home from, of all things, *vacation*.

He shut the door to his corner office and sat in his leather chair with a sigh. He stared at the twenty or so emails waiting for his attention and grimaced. He clicked open the first one and dealt with the routine security problem someone else should have handled *before* it got to him.

He lifted his mug to his lips, frowning as the lukewarm coffee slipped down his throat.

Yup. Shitty day, all right. Sometimes living mortal is a real pain in the ass.

***

Grimm watched as his youngest child left his office.

What a disappointment he's turned out to be.

He'd given the boy a simple enough task. Kill Baldur and Loki. It shouldn't have taken centuries, but somehow time had slipped away from them, and the two banes of his existence were still running around attempting to wreak havoc.

Baldur required nothing more than to be pierced through the heart with something crafted of mistletoe. Loki, admittedly, was more difficult, with his ability to heal much faster than expected, his shapeshifting abilities, and most of all, his daughter, Hel.

But you'd think, after a millennium, Vali would have gotten it right. The boy's penchant for toying with his intended victims was becoming more and more of a liability.

Grimm sighed and stroked the stone heads of the paired ravens sitting on his desk. Now that all of the players were in place, it was possible he would be able to take both his prodigal son and bastard blood brother out in one fell swoop, ending forever their threat to his rule of the Aesir.

All it would take would be a judicious use of his special weapon, a little trickery, and a lot of fast-talking.

All of which he had in spades. He smiled grimly at the cases of weapons lining one wall of his office, part of his "collection" of antiquities. He got up, opened the case closest to the desk, and pulled out the long spear. It was perfectly preserved, the shaft solid and warm in his grasp, the head sharp and deadly. With a simple thought the spear lit up, flaring brightly.

After all, he was still Odin.

Chapter Two

Jordan Grey rolled her eyes at the passionate clinch the two people on the screen were in. Her secretary, on the other hand, sighed blissfully.

"I have waited so long for you, my darling."

"And I you, my sweet."

"If not for your husband we would be man and wife now."

"I know, Vincente, I know!"

"Oh, Gloria!"

"Oh, Vincente!"

"Oh my stomach." The snort of laughter from the red-haired man sitting on the couch was nearly drowned out by Jamie's outraged squawk. Jordan put her hands on her hips. "Didn't I tell you no more dubbed foreign soaps in the office?"

"It's a classic!" Jamie spun around in her chair and glared at her boss.

Jordan stared at the overly mustached, mullet-haired "hero". He had the blonde, overly hair-sprayed heroine in a clinch that could only be deemed terrifying. It looked like they were licking each other's tongues. "It's nauseating."

"It's sweet."

"No. Roses are sweet. Chocolate is sweet. This is…" She squinted, staring in horrified disbelief at the office screen. "Are those gold lamé briefs?" She shook her head. "That man is wearing gold lamé *briefs*!"

Jamie spun around in her chair so fast Jordan's head spun. "Really?"

"Ew. You know he's old enough to be your father, right?"

"Not in this he's not. In this, Vincente is *hot*." Jamie fanned her face, her expression wicked.

"Jamie. Gold lamé briefs are. Not. Hot. *Ever*."

"Speak for yourself."

She pinched the bridge of her nose. "For the love of God, make it go away."

"Actually, I think Vincente is pretty hot, too."

Jordan glared at Jeff, who ducked behind the book he'd been reading. "And everyone knows what great taste in men *you* have." She turned back to Jamie. "Turn it off." She sighed when Jamie, with a pout, complied. "That's better."

"God, you are such a bitch." Jeff laughed, peeking over the book he'd been reading.

She smirked at him. "Takes a bitch to know a bitch, bitch."

"Aw, c'mon, Jordan! The love scene was coming up. Pleeeaase?"

Jamie had her hands clasped in front of her, her very finest imitation of innocence plastered all over her face. Jordan looked at Jamie over the top of pretend glasses, deepening her voice to match that of her stepfather, and the twins' father, Fred Grimm. "It is undignified for a grown woman to beg."

"Like Dad doesn't make your mom beg *every* night." Jeff smirked at Jordan's look of horror.

"*Ew*!" Her brother and sister laughed as she stuck her fingers in her ears, scrunched her eyes shut and started yelling, "Lalalalalala," at the top of her lungs. She'd never do something like that with clients in the office, but it was lunchtime, so she knew the place was empty. Besides, who else could she cut loose with but the Wonder Twins?

Jordan opened her eyes, ready to laugh, startled when she saw Jamie shaking her head. She stopped mid-"la". Jeff's mouth was hanging open in horrified amusement.

Oh, no. Clients. I look like an idiot in front of clients. Crap. Travis is gonna kill me.

Jordan turned and saw the two most gorgeous men she'd ever seen in her life standing in her doorway.

I look like an idiot in front of hot clients. Double-crap.

The dark-haired one was obviously laughing at her. The wickedest smile she'd ever seen rested on a pair of full, sensual lips. Dark eyes danced as she slowly removed her fingers from her ears. He had a small gold nose ring marring an otherwise perfect nose. He was a full head taller than her in her heeled boots, and half a head taller than his companion, with broad shoulders encased in black leather. Ripped, dark blue jeans encased muscular legs, leading down to a pair of black sneakers. Rich, dark red hair tumbled around his head, making him look like he'd just crawled out of bed.

Bad boy alert.

Jordan was a sucker for bad boys. She could feel the saliva pooling in her mouth as her gaze traveled back up his legs, pausing at the impressive package outlined by his jeans, to that wide chest and back to his face. She felt her cheeks heat as he stared back with a hot, knowing look.

Embarrassed to be caught staring like a lusty teenager, she turned her direction to his companion.

Oh. My. God.

The blond next to him was…was…words failed her at the other vision of ultimate hotness standing before her. Long, pale blond hair cascaded down to just brush his shoulders. Blue eyes the color of forget-me-nots were wide open as he obviously fought off a laugh. His upper lip formed a perfect cupid's bow, something that should have looked feminine. On him, it just made her want to lick to see if he tasted as good as he looked. His full lower lip trembled with his efforts not to laugh. He was broad shouldered and muscular under his black suede coat. He, too, wore blue jeans and black sneakers, but where on the redhead they played up his dangerous looks, on the blond it was like wrapping paper on a present. She just wanted to rip into it and see what was underneath.

Apart, they were incredible. Together, they were enough to stun the most jaded of feminine eyes. She had the urge to stamp her name across each of their foreheads before anyone else got a look at them.

Angel and demon, eh?

A brief vision of her between the two of them, light and dark, yin and yang, flashed through her mind. She squished it before it could go too far and get her in trouble.

Make that double trouble. "Welcome to Guardian Investigations. Can I help you gentlemen?" She nearly sighed in relief at the professional, only slightly breathless tone she managed.

"We're here to see Jordan Grey."

Jordan held back a shiver as the deep voice of the redhead washed over her. He had a slight accent that slurred his es's a little bit. "I'm Jordan Grey."

The two men exchanged a look she couldn't decipher. "See? I told you she'd be perfect."

The blond rolled his eyes and turned back to her. "We need your help." The blond had the same accent.

Jordan sighed. *Damn. Definitely clients.* Which meant Demon Boy and Archangel were off-limits. *Double damn.* She waved them into her office, glad that the twins were already maneuvering to leave. "Pleased to meet you. Is there anything my staff can get you before we sit down and discuss your case?"

"Coffee, if you don't mind." The redhead sauntered in and sat on one of the chairs in front of her desk.

The blond followed, smiling at Jeff, who practically drooled all over him. The blond sat in the other chair and turned that devastating smile on Jamie. "Water, please, thank you."

His double-u sound was a cross between a double-u and a vee, and suddenly she placed the accent. After all, she heard it every day. She smiled. "Are you two Norwegian?"

They turned and looked at each other, then back at her. "Yes. How did you know?"

She smiled broadly as she sat behind her desk. "My father has the same accent."

"We—" the blond cut off as the redhead elbowed him, hard, "—need your help."

She nearly frowned at the obvious gesture. Blondie had meant to say something else. Something like, *We know*, perhaps?

"Logan Saeter." The redhead stood halfway, holding out his hand.

Jordan shook it briefly and turned to the blond, who stood completely. "Kiran Tait." That devastating smile was still on his lips, warm and inviting. "Call me Kir."

"Pleased to meet you. How can I help you gentlemen?"

They waited until Jamie brought in the coffee and water, shutting the door behind her, before Logan spoke. "We need to prove that Oliver Grimm attempted to murder Kir and frame me for it."

Jordan couldn't keep the shock out of her voice. "Excuse me?"

"He's telling the truth."

Jordan stared at Kir. Kir stared back. He looked like he was *willing* her to believe Logan. "Oliver Grimm, head of Grimm and Sons?"

Kir nodded. Logan looked amused.

Jordan stood. "I'm sorry, gentlemen, but I don't think I can help you."

Logan snorted. He turned to Kir and grinned. "She thinks she can't help us."

Kir frowned at Logan. "Shush." He turned back to Jordan and smiled that angel's smile. "We know Grimm is like your grandfather. It's why we wanted to work with you. If we can get you to believe us, perhaps we have a chance of proving it to the rest of the world."

She stared at him like he'd just grown another perfect head on those perfect shoulders. "Are you freakin' insane?"

He blinked, looking startled as her voice went from cultured smoothness to a rough Philly accent in two seconds flat. Logan snickered, his expression delighted as Jordan lit into them with both barrels.

"He's my *grandfather*."

"Step-grandfather."

"*Doesn't matter!* Hello? Conflict of interest here!"

"That's the whole point. If someone with your ethics believes us, and can *prove* it, we'll be able to see to it that Grimm is punished for what he's done."

She looked back and forth between the two of them, angel and demon, and wondered if they were actually telling the truth. Logan had a smirk on his face, but he still managed to look viciously determined. Kir looked...hopeful. Like his fate rested in her hands. Add in that Oliver Grimm was a cold son-of-a-bitch who scared the bejesus out of her, and...

Fuck. Kir blinked, the wistful hope on his face tugging at her heart. *Puppy dog eyes. I'm screwed.* She was a total sucker, and she knew it. She sighed and sat down. "Tell me your story." *Man, I am so gonna regret this...*

***

Kir grinned. *Yes!* They'd gotten her to hear them out. Now, if he could curb Logan's natural instinct to yank people's chains, they might get her to agree to help them.

"I have an…unusual tale to tell. Do you like mythology, Ms. Grey?"

The look on Logan's face was priceless. One brow rose as he turned to Kir with a *What the hell are you doing?!?* expression. They'd talked strategy in the car on their way over to Jordan's office, and this *wasn't* what they'd discussed.

Fuck it. She'd learn the truth sooner or later. To his mind, it was better to lay their cards on the table before things went too far.

And if that didn't work, there was always Logan's back-up plan. Tying her up and carting her off, whether she liked it or not, held a certain appeal. He tamped down his urge to do just that, explanations be damned.

What is wrong with me? He'd never, in all their long years together, even been attracted to anyone other than Logan, but the small, curvy woman seated behind her desk drew like no other being had since…well, since Logan.

"Mythology?"

The slow way she drawled it, sitting back in her seat with a blank look, said it all. She had her voice back under control, too, the smooth, anchorman, androgynous accent back in place. Odds were good that, after his story, they'd be falling back on Plan B. He held back a shiver of lust with difficulty, keeping his gaze off Logan. There was nothing he wanted more than Logan's happiness, and it would kill Logan if he saw desire for another person on Kir's face. "Yes, Ms. Grey. Mythology. Norse mythology in particular."

Her gaze darted to Logan and back to him. Those wide, dark brown eyes were carefully blanked. He viewed that with regret. They'd been lovely filled with her laughter. He wondered briefly what they would look like full of passion, or languorous with sated lust. "Okay, I'll bite. What bit of Norse mythology should I become acquainted with?"

"The bit where Loki was directly responsible for the death of Baldur."

"I'm familiar with that myth, yes."

The careful way she was wording her responses wasn't encouraging. "I thought so." He leaned forward, hands clasped between his knees. "I want you to think about the myth, if you don't mind."

"Okay."

"Baldur was invulnerable to all substances, save mistletoe, which was, at the time, too young a plant to give its word not to harm him. Loki supposedly discovered this, handed the blind god Hodr a dart or arrow tipped in mistletoe, and guided his hand. Baldur died as the mistletoe pierced his heart. Loki fled as the gods killed Hodr for Baldur's death.

"Hel claimed she was willing to release Baldur back into the world if every living being cried, mourning him. But the gods found one holdout, a witch named Pokk, who was supposedly Loki in disguise. Pokk refused to weep. Hel held Baldur in her grasp and refused to let him go. When the gods realized they'd been tricked they returned to the cave, determined to exact revenge. Pokk fled into the back of the cave, turned into a raven, and flew off into the night. Eventually the gods tracked Loki down, tied him to a mountain with the entrails of his own son, there to writhe in torment until Ragnarok." He turned to Logan. "Did I miss anything?"

"Nanna's death."

Kir winced. "Right. The goddess Nanna, on hearing of her spouse's death and the failure of the gods to bring him back to life, committed suicide." And it galled him to say the lie. There was no way Nanna would have killed herself. Grimm had murdered her to protect his secrets, and whatever she'd known had died with her. And going to Hel and trying to speak to the dead was an exercise in futility.

"Right. So, now that our cultural anthropology lesson is done, what does this have to do with my grandfather?"

He ignored Logan, who was shaking his head in disbelief. That sardonic look was back on his face. From the relaxed way he sat, hands crossed over his stomach, Kir knew his lover was ready for anything. Logan always looked the most relaxed just before he sprang into action. "Have you ever wondered how much truth there was in the old myths?"

She leaned forward in her chair. Her elbow landed on the desk as she rested her chin in her palm. "Not particularly, no."

"All right. Think like a detective, then."

She smiled. "Yes, that will be *so* difficult for me."

Her sarcastic drawl had his eyes narrowing. *Damn, she's asking for it.*

Part of him wanted to give it to her, too. He eyed Logan sideways, not surprised to see his lover's eyes narrowed on him. He turned his attention back to the woman seated behind the desk and ordered his cock to stand down.

"If you're familiar with Loki then you're familiar with his ability to shift shape, right?"

"Yes."

"Are you familiar with the fact that the *only* form Loki couldn't shift into was a bird?"

She looked thoughtful. "No."

"He had to borrow Frejya's cloak to do it." He nodded towards her computer. "If you like, I'll wait a moment while you verify that."

She shook her head, frowning. "No, that's okay. I believe you." It was obvious she had no idea where he was going, or how all of this tied into Grimm.

"So if Loki couldn't turn into a bird without Frejya's cloak, how did he, as Pokk, turn into a raven in the back of the cavern and fly away from the gods?"

She opened her mouth and then closed it, clearly stunned. "I...don't know."

"And whose bird is the raven?"

"Odin, of course." She blinked, a frown crossing her face. "Wait. Are you saying *Odin* framed Loki?"

Kir shrugged. "Odin is a shapeshifter. He's always been associated with lies and trickery."

She tilted her head, her gaze narrowing on him. "Is?"

She's sharp. Good. He nodded. *Now for the difficult part; convincing her that myth and reality are a lot more closely related than she thinks.* "Is."

She sat back, her hand flopping down onto the top of her desk with a thunk. "You think you're Baldur?"

"No." He smiled when her shoulders sagged in relief. "I *am* Baldur." Or was. As far as he was concerned, Baldur died that day, staring down at a bleeding man, filled with the knowledge that his father wanted him dead. Had, in fact, succeeded in killing his brother.

She closed her eyes and pinched the bridge of her nose. "Let me guess." She waved her hand blindly in Logan's direction. "And he's Loki, right?"

"Yes."

She opened her eyes and glared at them both. "Very funny. Ha ha." She stood and pointed to the door. "Get out."

Logan stood and stuck his hands in his pocket. "Plan B, blondie?"

"Not yet." Kir stood as well, watching Jordan carefully. "We can prove it, you know."

Logan grimaced. "Uh-oh. Is she done enough for Plan A1?"

He ignored Logan's mutter and concentrated on the woman in front of him. "Would you like us to prove it?"

She put her hands on her hips and grinned, full of cocky assurance, that accent of hers bleeding through the sophisticated façade. "Sure, go ahead. Prove he's a fire giant and you're an invulnerable god, and I'll work for you. Hell, I'll do it for free."

Logan's grin was full of demonic delight. "Bargain made." He winked at Kir, waiting for him to make the first move.

Kir shrugged. "Okay." He picked up her dagger-like letter opener, put his hand on her desk, and stabbed as hard as he could at his hand. The metal bent sideways with an audible screech, refusing to touch his skin.

That made her gasp. Logan's trick, however, made her scream. After all, it wasn't every day you watched a man made out of fire clean his fingernails with a bent letter opener.

Her shriek brought her coworkers running, nearly knocking a quickly human Logan onto his ass. Kir held up the bent, blackened blade of the dagger-like letter opener. "Believe us now?"

Logan watched Jordan blanch and almost felt sorry for her. He hated when Kir pulled this last-minute surprise kind of shit, but they'd done it Logan's way before and look how far he'd gotten them. Nowhere, which sucked the big fat hairy one. This time, Kir had insisted he be the one to get the ball rolling.

Too bad he'd had to pull out the friggin' catapult to do it.

He watched Jordan sink into her seat, her pretty, dark chocolate eyes wide and blank. He took his time, enjoying the sight of all those curves bouncing as she landed hard.

She reached up one hand and tugged on her earring in a defensive gesture that had Logan fighting not to go to her.

It had been a very long time since someone other than Kir caught his interest. And it would add all sorts of complications to an already complicated situation, if Kir's reaction to her was anything to go by. Unless he missed his guess, his lover wanted her, too, and was fighting it with everything in him. With anyone else, it would have worked, too. Kir had become a master at hiding his true feelings. But there was no way he could hide them from Logan.

He turned back and studied the woman he knew was going to change their lives, whether they wanted it or not. Tousled dark brown hair his fingers itched to stroke framed a long, narrow face with full, pouty lips. Dark slacks hugged a sweetly rounded ass, and a pink summer sweater caressed her generous breasts. Low-heeled black boots added an illusion of height she just didn't have. She looked like a corporate casual secretary, someone who could pass just about anywhere without notice, which was undoubtedly what she wanted people to see.

She was smart, she was funny, and she was cute as a button. And he was doomed. Her father was going to rip his gonads off and stuff them down his throat if he found out the thoughts Logan was entertaining about his baby girl. And if her stepfather found out… He winced, knowing *exactly* what her stepfather would do to him.

Hell, Kir they'd probably welcome with open arms. Kir's lover? Only if it involved red-hot pokers and bamboo shoots.

Kir put the bent blade back down and sat, ignoring the two other people in the room as they babbled. He crossed his ankles, watching the pandemonium around them with a serene smile.

The smug bastard. It was a good thing he was so cute.

When Kir looked over at him and winked, Logan nearly laughed out loud.

"It was a parlor trick, really. I only *thought* he'd stabbed his hand."

Jordan's explanation seemed to calm her coworkers. It hadn't occurred to either of them to look for a stab mark in the wood, or why the blade had bent rather than sticking (or why it was blackened, either), but apparently they were willing to buy an obvious line of bullshit rather than see the truth. Humans had a habit of seeing only what they wanted to see. Hell, they were completely ignoring the scorched carpet and the smell of smoke, too, although the redheaded guy was giving all three of them some mighty strange looks. He'd have to keep an eye on that one.

The two finally left, sending worried glances over their shoulders on their way out the door. Logan reached back and closed it behind them, grinning at the faint, outraged squawk the short, curly-haired redhead (Jenny? Jamie?) let out.

She let go of her earring and focused on Kir. "You're Baldur." She scrubbed her face with both hands when he nodded. Her attention turned to him, and Logan felt his dick twitch in a surge of lust. "You're Loki?"

He bowed from his seat, knowing how arrogant he looked and not giving a fuck. If she couldn't deal with him the way he was, well…she would just have to get used to it.

"And you want to prove that Oliver Grimm, God, I can't believe I'm saying this, framed you for the murder of Kir, who is Baldur. Which means that Grimm would be Odin."

"By Odin, I think she's got it!"

That earned him a glare from two sets of eyes. He grinned, pleased when Kir chuckled. "Asshole."

He thought about answering, "Later, dear" but decided Jordan had had enough surprises for one day.

"If Grimm is Odin, who is my father?"

Logan sat up a little straighter. "Are you sure you want the answer to that question?"

She rolled her eyes. "You've already blown my world apart. What else can you do to me?"

Lots of things, little girl. Lots of things. He cleared his throat and tried to block out the image of her bent over her desk, Kir's cock between those sweet, strawberry colored lips, while he fucked her hard from behind. *Kir and I are going to have to have a long talk about this.* Not for anything would he hurt Kir. "Frey."

"Fred is Frey?"

"No. Fred is Thor. Your biological father, Adam, is Frey."

It came out a little harsher than he'd intended; visions of her naked and wanting made his voice gruff with lust. Her face turned whiter, if that was possible. He was beginning to become seriously concerned that she'd pass out, a vision that turned off the sexy fantasies he'd been having ever since he and Kir had entered her office. He stood and marched around the desk, ready to catch her if she fell, every one of his protective instincts going into overdrive.

Kir mirrored his movements on her other side, his own concern obvious. Kir rested one hand on the back of her chair, the other on her desk. "You didn't have to blurt it out like that, Logan."

"How the hell else do you tell someone that their father is a god? 'Hi, honey, here's some flowers and chocolates, oh by the way your dad throws lightning bolts at mortals for shits and giggles'?"

"My mom?"

Both men blinked and looked down at her croaked words. "What?"

"Is my mom a goddess?"

He exchanged a look with Kir, who shrugged. "No." He had to swallow to stop himself from tacking on "sweetheart".

Oh, yeah. So doomed. He looked down into her sweetly stubborn face and sighed. *But what a way to go.*

Chapter Three

Jordan sat in the passenger seat of Kir's cherry red Mustang and tried to process everything the two men had told her, and shown her, in her office. They'd insisted she wasn't capable of driving, and, from how lightheaded she still felt, she had to agree with them.

Okay. So, Dad is Frey. Mom is mortal. Grey, Frey...nobody said Dad was the brightest bulb in the chandelier.

If Dad is Frey, and mom is human, what the hell does that make me? And does Mom know? What about Jamie and Jeff? Or Magnus and Morgan? Are they full gods? Two sets of twins, one half mortal, the other...what?

God, my head hurts. She almost chuckled out loud at the irony of that phrase.

She rubbed her aching head and saw Kir glance at her. She ignored it, still trying to puzzle out who knew what, or, hell, who *was* what.

Logan, on the other hand, was more difficult to ignore. He reached forward and rubbed the back of her neck, the touch warm and surprisingly soothing. "Ease up, Jordan. I know it's a lot to take in, but we're willing to answer any questions you have."

"And we're ordering in pizza." Kir's cheerful announcement fell flat as Logan and Jordan stared at him. "What? I'm just saying."

Jordan stared at Logan's reflection in the rearview mirror and quirked her eyebrows. Kir had been determinedly cheerful the entire twenty minute drive from her office to their condo. "He has a great future at Hallmark, doesn't he?"

Logan choked, hiding his laugh behind the back of his hand. Kir, on the other hand, reached out and gently bopped her on the back of the head. "Very funny. Ha ha." He pointed towards the backseat. "And you, stop encouraging her."

"Yes, Your Highness." Logan did another one of his bows. His laughing gaze tangled with Kir's in the mirror before they both looked away with identical grins.

Jordan watched the exchange with a puzzled frown. She could have sworn both men had been looking at her in her office with something other than professional interest. However, having a brother who was gay, she'd learned to recognize the signs of two men who were a couple. And from the looks of things, Kir and Logan were definitely a couple.

She saw Logan staring at her again in the rearview mirror, confusing her even further. He was looking at her like she was a Godiva chocolate and he was starving for a taste. *What the hell?*

Then she thought about all of the myths about Loki, and Loki's sexuality. If the myths were true, Loki was firmly bisexual. *Trisexual? Omnisexual? The man is a* mom, *for God's sake! Do they even* have *a word for Loki's sexuality?* From the quirky grin that briefly passed over his face he knew exactly what she was thinking about, too. She faced forward again, her cheeks heating in embarrassment. Pictures of the two men wrapped in each other's arms danced through her head. She firmly squashed them, not wanting to deal with the consequences of her fantasies. She didn't exactly carry around spare panties, for God's sake.

Jordan didn't do "casual sex". As far as she was concerned, there was nothing *casual* about it. Unless her emotions were engaged, her body wasn't. Although, from the feel of Logan's fingers still stroking her neck, her body was more than willing to drag her emotions along for the ride. *Oh, and what a ride it would be,* her traitorous body whispered.

Kir pulled into their condo's parking garage and pulled into the space assigned to them. He started to get out of the car and was stopped by Logan's grip on his shoulder.

"No, Kir." Logan got out of the car with a grunt and took a look around the garage.

Kir rolled his eyes. "Sit, Kir. Stay, Kir. Good dog. Woof."

"What's he doing?" Jordan watched as Logan scoped out the place, his movements sleek and sure. She bet he didn't make a single sound as he moved. He looked right and left, leaning behind a pillar to check out the lower level. His jeans tightened across his damn fine ass. Her body knelt and pled at the feet of her emotions, *Please? Pretty please? With a cherry on top?*

"Making sure there are no assassins waiting for us."

Jordan blinked and focused back on Kir. *My God, that much gorgeous should come with a warning label.* "Assassins?"

Kir nodded as he watched Logan move around the parking lot. "Grimm wants me dead in the worst way. He has an assassin named Val—"

"Oh no. Uncle Val?" Talk about a libido killer. Uncle Val *looked* scary as hell, but he'd always been affectionate towards her and the twins.

Kir glanced at her but quickly turned his attention back to a rapidly approaching Logan. "*Uncle* Val?"

"Brown hair, blue eyes, mean-looking son of a bitch?"

"That would be Val."

"Yup. Uncle Val."

"Uncle Val is Vali, the man who murdered my brother."

Jordan stared out the front windshield and searched her memory of Norse mythology, trying to match up the man who'd tossed her in the air as a child with the man Kir was describing. "Um. Vali?"

Kir sighed as Logan motioned for them to leave the car. "Wait until we get upstairs, okay?"

"Okay, what?" Logan asked as he held open Jordan's door.

"Okay, you guys are going to explain to me who Vali is once we get upstairs."

"Oh." Logan shook his head as he led them to the elevator. "Listen closely, because I hate talking like this and I'm not repeating it." He took a deep breath as they entered the elevator, and Jordan paused to admire how wide his chest was. And then, as the elevator began its rise to the twenty-second floor, he crossed his arms over that chest and began to chant.

"I saw for Baldur—
for the bloodstained sacrifice,
Odin's child—
the fates set hidden.
There stood full-grown,
higher than the plains,
slender and most fair,
the mistletoe.

"There formed from that stem
which was slender-seeming,
a shaft of anguish, perilous:
Hodr started shooting.
A brother of Baldur
was born quickly:

he started—Odin's son—
slaying, at one night old.

"He never washed hands,
never combed head,
till he bore to the pyre
Baldur's adversary—
while Frigg wept
in Fen Halls
for Valhall's woe.
Do you still seek to know? And what?"

***

Kir leaned back as Logan's deep voice washed over him. There were times he missed the cadence of the poetry of his homeland, but this particular piece was one of his least favorites. It described how, at one day old, Vali slew Hodr in retaliation for the death of Baldur. That Hodr was both blind and was meant to help Baldur rule Valhalla had factored in greatly when Grimm was making his plans to murder them both.

Jordan leaned back against the wall. "What was that?"

"It's a portion of the Poetic Edda, translated by Ursula Dronke." Logan was staring at her, his expression carefully nonchalant.

"Oh. Well. That clears *that* up." From the confused frown on her face, it had raised more questions than it answered.

The doors opened onto a hallway. Kir stepped out, pulling out his key card. Jordan stepped out next. Logan pushed passed her and Kir, taking Kir's key card to open the door to their condo. Since they'd come to Philadelphia Logan had been a nervous wreck, worried sick that Val and Grimm would find them before they would have a chance to set their plans in motion.

He entered the posh condo, his sneakers making no sound on the shiny maple flooring. Kir sighed as Logan nodded, letting him know no one had disrupted the wards Logan had set before heading out that morning.

Without missing a beat Jordan sat on the modern, snow white chaise. "Okay, I have to admit, the knife thing wasn't nearly as impressive as flaming Logan." She grinned, letting them know she was completely aware of the double entendre.

"Very funny." Logan flopped down next to her, one knee resting on the white chaise, his elbow resting along the back and his hand propping up his head as he faced her.

Kir took a seat on the ottoman that doubled as a coffee table and picked up the explanation they'd begun in the elevator. "So Vali, at one day old, killed my brother."

"Precocious little tyke."

"Yeah, he was a total Gerber baby." Logan sneered.

"Why didn't Hodr just, I don't know, stop him?"

"Because, unlike a normal baby, Vali grew to manhood in the space of a few hours. He couldn't stop Vali from killing him."

"He couldn't see where Vali was, couldn't fight him, and felt that his death was completely justified." Kir heard the old pain in Logan's voice; Hodr hadn't meant anything to him at the time, but Baldur's grief over his dead brother and anger at his traitorous father had been the first stepping stone in the beginning of their relationship. For the first time, he'd seen Logan as someone other than an angry, annoying young god, and Logan had seen Kir as more than the pretty, admired, social butterfly.

"Can I ask you a quick question that's been bothering me?"

Kir nodded. "Of course."

"Should I call you guys Baldur and Loki?"

"No!"

"Uh-uh."

They looked at each other and grimaced. They'd both replied at the same time and the same volume.

"We'd prefer to be called by the names we've chosen rather than the names that were chosen for us." Kir turned his attention back to a confused looking Jordan. "We're no longer those people."

Her gaze intensified as she worked out what he meant. "You mean you're not a god of spring and he's not a fire giant?"

"I'm not a naive, trusting fool and he's not a hormonal teenager. Ow." Kir rubbed the spot on his thigh Logan smacked.

"Hormonal teenager?"

"You fucked anything that would let you, and I mean *anything*, and you emo'd all over the place." He looked at Jordan and grinned. "His growing pains were *horrendous*."

"I did *not* 'emo'!"

Kir laughed at the outrage in Logan's voice. He'd curled his fingers up, making quotation marks.

"Oh, really? How about the dinner party where you got drunk and told everyone off, including letting some of the gods know that their darling, chaste wives were off playing in the clover while their husbands were at war, hmm?"

Logan snorted. "Those idiots weren't off making war, they were rolling around in their own clover."

Jordan's bemused voice interrupted them. "Did you know, with the nose ring, every time you snort I think of a bull?"

Kir had to bury his face in the ottoman, but couldn't do anything about his shaking shoulders, or the muffled sounds of his laughter.

Out of the corner of his eye he saw Jordan put her hands on her hips. "Okay. If you two are done playing, can you actually explain to me how this all went down?"

***

Logan watched as Jordan stood and began pacing in front of the floor to ceiling windows that looked out over Rittenhouse Square. He ignored the still muffled sounds of Kir's laughter. It was both annoying and endearing that, once his lover got going, getting him to stop was damn near impossible. He had to work it out of his system in his own time. Unfortunately, that left Logan to explain everything to Jordan.

"I was watching Odin fairly closely at the time, for some reason or another. I think I was planning on playing a prank on Frigg and wanted to make sure he wasn't going to get in my way. I saw him leave early one morning and something about the way he left, his face, maybe his body language, let me know he was up to no good."

"You followed him?"

"Of course. I had to know what would make him look like that, like the cat that got the cream. I figured this was much better than playing a silly trick on Frigg." Jordan also ignored Kir as he sat up and wiped the laughter tears away. "I saw Odin shift shape into me and pick a sprig of mistletoe in full view of a farmer. I made sure he didn't see me as he took off again, heading back home.

"I knew mistletoe was Baldur's only vulnerability, so I was curious as to why his father would be picking some, especially since he'd taken my form to do it." His smile was sour. "Not exactly confidence inducing. Anyway, I followed Odin and watched him. He crafted the sprig of mistletoe into an arrowhead and made an arrow meant to kill his own son."

"Why didn't you say anything?"

He stared at her. "You're kidding, right? Who would have believed me?"

"I didn't believe him." Kir sighed. "My own father, out to kill me? It was unbelievable."

"So I managed to subdue Baldur, tied him up, and put him in a safe place where he could watch what happened and no one would know. Then I took his shape and his place."

"How did you keep from getting injured by the things they fired at you?"

"He didn't."

Damn. Kir still *hasn't gotten over that?* The anguish in Kir's voice was noticeable to anyone who knew him. Without thought he rubbed his lover's knee, soothing him, not surprised when Kir picked his hand up, squeezed it, and let it go.

He turned his attention back to Jordan. "I took it, and let them think it didn't hurt."

"But… I thought the Norse gods could die?"

"We can, but on the way I'd had a little chat with my daughter. She agreed that, for that short amount of time, no amount of damage, not even an instantly fatal wound, would kill me."

"Your daughter?"

He looked her straight in the eyes. "I had three children outside my marriage, remember?"

She gulped. "Hel."

He nodded. "So I stood there, and managed to keep them all from seeing my bleeding using a spell an old Jotun witch had taught me. Odin shifted into me and strode onto the field."

"That's when I knew Logan was telling the truth."

He let the silence linger for a moment after Kir's soft announcement before continuing. The agony of that day, the barbs and arrows piercing his flesh while he smiled and laughed it off, still had the power to awaken him with nightmares not even Kir could soothe. "So Odin, as me, stood behind Hodr, handed his blind son the arrow meant to kill his heir, and shot me instead, right through the heart. He then took off, making sure to shift back into himself out of sight of the others so he could properly express his outrage." He smiled cynically. "To celebrate, he immediately rushed off and fucked his mistress, begetting Vali in the process, who slew Hodr, etc., etc."

Kir grimaced. "I watched as Loki was borne off, his body anointed for burial. As soon as he could he left a simulacrum in his place and released me, but he collapsed before he could do anything more. He was so wounded, pierced so many times that I thought, despite his daughter's promises, he would die."

"So Baldur took it upon himself to go to Hel and explain what had happened, never knowing that Frigg had sent a messenger asking her to release him back into the world."

Kir shrugged. "You would have done the same." Kir was right. Logan would have. "The messenger arrived shortly after I did. Hel and I had to think fast; she decided to pretend I was dead, and I had to go along with it. She came up with the fiction of having the world weep for me, thinking that would buy us some time and explain my miraculous return."

"But we hadn't counted on Odin."

Jordan sat on the edge of the ottoman, her thigh brushing Kir's. She frowned, obviously lost in thought, not noticing the way Kir swallowed or how his jeans slowly began to fill out as his cock leapt to life.

Kir glanced at Logan, guilt flashing across his face before he carefully inched his leg away from Jordan's.

Logan smiled. *Damn. I thought so. We need to talk once we send her on her way.* "Odin turned himself into Pokk, refused to weep, and flew off, insuring neither Baldur nor Hodr would ever grace the world again."

"And insuring that Loki's days were numbered, as well."

"I had no idea what Hel and Baldur had done. I'd taken myself off to heal, spending some time in a pond as a salmon. That's where they found me. They took me, bound me to three slabs of stone with the enchanted entrails of my own child and left me there to rot under the venom of that damn snake." Logan could feel his fists clenching in his lap at the thought of his murdered child.

"What happened to your other son, the one that wasn't killed?"

Logan shook his head. "I don't know what happened to Nari. We were never able to find him. We can only assume that Odin killed him, too."

It was Kir's turn to rub Logan's knee soothingly. "But I came back and freed him. Sigyn wanted us to inform the world what had happened, but Loki and I agreed that that would be too dangerous for all of us. By that point, Nanna was dead, and we were worried the same fate would befall Sigyn if she openly helped us. Besides, we had to prove to the other gods, beyond a shadow of a doubt, that Loki was innocent. At the time, all of them were firmly on Odin's side, especially when he informed them that I would return after Ragnarok to lead them into an era of peace."

"They turned Baldur into a risen god and me into the harbinger of their deaths." Logan's smile didn't waver as Jordan stared at him. "We waited, and waited, for the right opportunity to present itself, but every time we made a move, Odin somehow found out and sicced Vali on us."

"Thought and Memory." Jordan's tone was thoughtful; she was processing the information.

She's smart. She's figured out how he keeps finding us. Damn. He had a thing for people with smarts. "Among others."

"And now, if you so much as show yourselves before the other gods, they think that it's some sort of sick, twisted trick."

"And Kir and I get to go into hiding for another century or two until they call off the hunt."

"What made you decide now was the time to try again?"

"Things have changed." Kir got up and went to the fridge, pulling out three colas. He brought each of them a can and popped the top on his. "Recently the gods themselves began to change. They've adapted amazingly well to technology. Some of them have even taken mortal wives, not all of whom know who their husbands really are."

"Like my mom?"

"Exactly."

"You think that, because they've integrated with mortal society, it's mellowed them out?"

Her skepticism was clear in her tone of voice. "No. I think they won't have any choice but to believe us when we present them with irrefutable proof, done in such a way that, no matter where they are on this earth, they'll see it."

"And my job is to convince them, with *irrefutable* proof, that you're innocent—" she pointed to Logan, then swung around to Kir, "—and you're alive?"

They looked at each other. Logan smirked. "Yup."

"That about covers it." Kir smiled sweetly at Jordan. "Should I order the pizza now?"

***

They are certifiably crazy. Then again, after the life they've been forced to live, who wouldn't be?

Jordan took a last bite of pizza and wiped her fingers off on a paper towel Kir had brought from the kitchen. Part of her was dying to explore the luxurious, modern condo.

It had been like stepping into her dream home, complete with pale blue walls and stunning views. "Okay. I have a couple of ideas on how to proceed, but you need to know how I operate." Logan grinned, and her pulse leapt. *Down, girl.* "Business-wise, perv."

"You say that like it's a bad thing."

She ignored Logan's mutter and focused on Kir, who was desperately trying not to laugh again. "We need to be really aggressive here. I'm not going to pull my punches with either one of you, and I don't expect you to pull your punches with me. If you disagree with something I'm doing, that's fine. Tell me." She turned to Logan again. "Then expect me to tell you to back off and let me do my job."

Both men frowned at that. "Don't expect us to allow you to put yourself in danger."

Surprised, she turned to Kir. "Wow. I would have expected that caveman attitude more from Logan, not you."

"He's a fierce mother bear when his cubs are endangered." Logan leaned back on the sofa, a smug look of satisfaction on his face.

Kir rolled his eyes and pointedly ignored him. "I mean it. If there seems to be the slightest threat to your safety, you pull back and regroup. Understood?"

"I'm a PI rather than a cop *because* I'm not into bodily harm. I don't like pain, pain hurts me."

"Didn't somebody famous say that first?" Logan looked at Kir, who looked back at him with a shrug.

"Daffy Duck, maybe?"

"I thought it was Rodney Dangerfield."

"Wait, wasn't it the Cowardly Lion?"

"Oh yeah, I think it was!"

"Are you two done?" Jordan glared at the two men who grinned at her unrepentantly. "Because this is serious, okay?"

"Of course it's serious. And we're serious that you are in no way to put yourself in danger." Kir's tone had gone from cheerfully playful to full of command in the space of a heartbeat. He looked at her like he expected her compliance on every level, and for a moment she saw the man who was truly meant to lead the gods.

The look of love and pride on Logan's face nearly brought tears to her eyes. His absolute faith and devotion to his lover was written all over his face.

Now I know they're telling the truth. No way could anyone, even Loki, fake that look.

She felt a momentary twinge of regret for what could have been with either of these men before she forced it down. Neither one was for her; they were for each other.

And then Kir ruined the moment. "Duh."

Jordan frowned. "Duh?"

Kir grinned as Logan collapsed with an exasperated sigh. "Duh. You find yourself in a position where you could get hurt you move. Val won't hold back from killing you, you know. Not if Grimm orders it."

Jordan rolled her eyes. "Yes, Mom."

"Do you carry a gun?"

Jordan snapped her fingers. "Damn. Left it at home with my fedora and trench coat."

"I'll take that as a no."

"You can take it any way you like." She tried to ignore the sudden heat in Kir's eyes, focusing on the problem at hand.

"How come Grimm hasn't just waltzed in here and blown both your heads off while you sleep?"

Loki grinned. "Simple. The wards."

"Wards?"

Logan wiggled his fingers at her. "Magic. Oooh."

She quickly ran through the miniscule amount of magical knowledge she had. Harry Potter and Lord of the Rings were about the extent of it. "What are wards?"

"Magical runes Logan puts up to prevent anyone from entering our home uninvited. They also protect us from magical prying eyes. They don't last forever, but they do the job long enough for us to realize our time is probably up and we should move on."

"Oh."

"Too much information?"

She frowned. "No, just wondering why they haven't figured out ways to counteract them before."

"They have." Logan smirked. "Then I change them."

"Change them? Isn't that supposed to be a bad thing? Didn't I read in some book somewhere that making up a new spell is, like, dangerous? On the level of *oops I melted the world?*"

"Not if you know what you're doing."

Kir smiled. "You need to remember something; Logan wasn't born Vanir or Aesir. He was born a Jotun."

"A what-un?"

"Jotun. A race of magical beings mistakenly called giants. To them, magic is an innate ability, not something you learn like a human wizard would have to. It has limits, of course, like the toll it takes on Logan's energy to do anything really complicated, but it gets the job done."

"Really? Wow." She filed that phrase *like a human wizard* away for later examination. She'd get more info on that at a better time. "Is there some way we can use Logan's magic to get your point across?" Before they could speak she winced. "No, wait, never mind. They'll all chalk it up to trickery again."

"Exactly."

She began to pace, her mind whirling a mile a minute. Plans were made and quickly discarded as she realized that most of what they could do would be viewed as just more of the same deceit they'd come to expect from Loki.

"What kind of powers do you have? I know all about the Human Torch here, but what can you do? Other than the bending knife trick?" She stared at Kir, eyes narrowed in thought.

He grinned. "Look out the window."

She turned and saw clouds begin to roll in on a perfectly sunny day. Dark clouds, fat with rain that began falling gently on the city below. "Rain. Huh. Anything else?" Thunder cracked, a shaft of lightning striking down somewhere outside the city. "Oh." She turned back to Kir, who had his head in his hands and was looking down at the floor. *Huh. Maybe it gives him a headache.* "I thought thunder and lightning were Thor's gig?"

Kir looked up. There was no trace of pain on his face. "It is, but as a God of Spring, I'm in charge of, um, April showers. You know, sudden thunderstorms? Thor's lightning is a lot more directed, more like a Zeus kind of thing."

"Huh." She looked outside; it was kind of pretty. She'd always liked thunderstorms. She flopped back down on the ottoman next to Kir and sighed, propping her chin on her hand, elbow on her knee. She looked over their heads and caught a glimpse of the laptop they'd set up on the glass dining room table. Why it was there instead of in the posh den she'd spied on the way in, she didn't know, but the sight gave her an idea of how to blend Kir's powers and Logan's in such a way that the Aesir couldn't ignore the message.

An evil grin crossed her face as she looked at the two very hot, very supernatural, very *photogenic*, men. "Have either of you heard of YouTube?"

***

Kir closed the door behind himself and Logan after having seen Jordan onto the elevator. He sighed and closed his eyes tightly, completely mortified.

Fuck. Logan saw my reaction to Jordan.

The knowing gleam in his lover's eyes did not bode well for the coming conversation.

So it was with some surprise he felt Logan gently push his hand into his hair, pulling Kir's mouth to his own. The kiss was a languid stroking of tongues, not the usual kiss Logan gave. Logan usually preferred hot, heavy kisses, full of passion and the promise of sex. This one was the kind of kiss Kir preferred. Soft, sweet, and full of the love they both felt.

"I love you, you know that, right?"

Kir focused on Logan's face. "No more than I love you."

"We need to talk."

Kir closed his eyes again, not wanting to see the pain in Logan's.

"Hey."

He sighed and moved past Logan's body and into the living room. Dejected, he sat on the sofa, his head in his hands. "I'm so sorry."

"For what? The fact that you're attracted to Jordan?"

Kir groaned.

"Kir." He looked up, surprised to see the understanding on Logan's face. "Me, too."

He felt a surprising flash of jealousy at that, but wasn't sure if it was for Logan or Jordan. *Not good...or very good?* "You want her, too?"

"Don't sound so surprised. She's a hell of a woman."

Kir found himself nodding his agreement. "She took everything we threw at her in stride."

"If I was her I would have kicked our asses out of my office, gone and had a few drinks, then convinced myself it never happened right after I called to have the carpet replaced."

"So what do we do about it?"

They stared into each other's faces, reading the promises they'd long ago made to each other and the new, sudden *want* they both felt. No matter how startlingly strong, there was no way Kir would act on it if it meant losing Logan.

Logan was his everything.

Kir reached out first, cupping Logan's cheek. "I would *never* do anything to hurt you, Logan."

"Ditto." Logan's face was flushed with pleasure, that demonic grin of his once again gracing his features.

"So, what do we do?"

He watched Logan slouch down onto the floor at his feet, resting his head against Kir's knees with a contented sigh. "The way I see it, we have two options."

"Those are?" Kir's heart rate picked up. He began absently stroking that fiery hair, wondering if Logan was thinking what he was thinking.

"Option one: we walk away from her once this is all over."

No!

The instant denial raced through his body, causing him to jump. *What the fuck?* He *never* had that reaction to losing anyone or anything…other than Logan.

It didn't help that Logan started to chuckle. "Thought so."

"Option two?"

His heart was in his throat right up until Logan looked up at him with a leer. "Don't you just love the French?"

Kir blinked. "Huh?"

"They come up with words for the most amazing concepts."

"Like?" Kir drawled. He was pretty sure now he knew where Logan was going, but he wanted confirmation before he said anything.

"Ménage a trois. It has such a sexy ring to it, doesn't it?"

"*Permanent* ménage?" The words had left his mouth before he even realized the significance of what he was saying. Something about Jordan just…felt *right*.

Logan's expression turned serious. "I'm not sure yet." He shook his head, smirking. "But tell me you aren't already a little in love with her, and I'll call you a liar. I mean, damn. She's got a smart mouth, hot body, bodacious ass, and she's clever as all hell. And she wants *both* of us."

Kir opened his mouth to say the words and found them stuck in his throat. "Damn."

"Ditto."

"How the hell did *that* happen?"

"I don't know, but it did." Logan was frowning again, this time in confusion. "It's like we've found something we didn't even know was missing. But if you asked, I would walk away from this. You know that." For the first time, Kir saw Logan's uncertainty peek through, reminding him of the broken man Loki had been after Baldur freed him from the mountain. The reckless youth he was had been burned away by the snake's acid, leaving behind a damaged man who tossed and turned at night, screaming denials as he relived everything over and over again. It had taken Kir a long time to ease his lover's torment. He also knew their relationship was the foundation the now confident, cocky man who was *still* inclined to take risks stood on.

Which was why he'd been so upset about his reaction to Jordan. But knowing that Logan felt the same eased that guilt

Kir thought about taking Jordan and making her theirs. Thanks to Logan's ability to shift genders as well as shape, Kir had been happily bisexual for centuries now. He'd felt no need to go outside the relationship when Logan could, literally, be everything and anything he needed. Logan, on the other hand, hadn't been able to explore that side of himself with Kir, since Kir couldn't change his shape. He knew that sometimes Logan longed for soft, scented flesh, rounded breasts and bellies, all of the things he'd given up when he'd pledged himself to Kir. But Logan, for all his wild youth and unhappy marriage, hadn't cheated on him once. And not once, through all of the long centuries, had either of them had the urge to add a third to their relationship.

Now, with the advent of one small, half-human woman, all of that was about to change. He could give the touch of a female back to his lover, *and* have them both for himself. He thought back to the odd feeling he'd had on the beach, that something was about to happen that would change them, and felt that sensation once more before it settled into a comfortable purr.

He saw the relief on Logan's face as he nodded his acceptance.

Jordan was theirs. Now they just had to seduce her to them.

Chapter Four

Logan was surprised to receive a phone call from Jordan two days later. "Hey, Logan, sorry I haven't gotten back in touch with you."

He leaned back in his chair, delighted to listen to the sound of her voice. She'd been unavailable for the last two days, despite numerous attempts to reach her, and he'd started to worry. "Where were you?"

There was a pause, and he just knew he'd sounded like a possessive idiot. "I was finishing up a case so I could concentrate on yours." He could hear the sounds of papers being shuffled around.

Logan frowned. "Was it dangerous?" Okay, make that a possessive and overly protective jerk. Way to win her trust, Saeter.

"No, Daddy. And I made sure to drink a full glass of juice this morning, too. I even took my vitamins."

If he had his way, that smart mouth of hers was going to get quite a workout. "How about if Daddy and Mommy come over and give Jordan a bath, hmm?"

She gasped.

"Do I get a kiss goodnight afterwards?"

"Logan!"

"Hey, you started it."

He was leering at the wall when Kir wandered into the office, his brows raised way up. "Is that Jordan?"

He punched the speaker button so Kir could listen in. "Yes, and she wants us to come over and—"

"Don't you dare, Logan Saeter!"

He laughed. "Oh, I'm in trouble now! She used my *full name!*"

Kir shook his head, his lips beginning to turn up in a grin.

"Smart ass." He could hear the laughter in her voice.

"Better a smart ass than a dumb ass."

"That whole line was asinine."

"Ooh, good one." He winked at Kir, who shook his head at him.

"The reason I called was to ask if you wanted to get together to go over the YouTube video."

Logan thought about what he'd have to do to get the condo ready for a date. Kir could clean while he got the makings for a meal. He looked over and saw Kir nodding as he headed out of the den. They'd been together long enough that they could practically read each other's minds. He smiled to himself when he heard Kir rummaging around in the closet where he kept all of his cleaning supplies. "I think we can swing that."

"What time?"

"Tonight, at seven?"

"Sounds good."

"Don't eat anything; we'll make it a dinner meeting." Logan knew one of the ways to a person's heart, male or female, was a well-cooked meal, and he planned on wowing her tonight. He picked up a pen and paper, all ready to write down what he'd need.

"More pizza? Yum! Especially if you order from the same place as last time."

Logan mentally rolled his eyes as he jotted down a quick menu. *You and Kir are going to get along just fine.* "I was thinking of cooking, actually."

There was silence for a moment. "Pizza's good."

One eyebrow twitched up in disbelief. "Hey, I'm a good cook."

"Um. Okay."

He frowned. "What's up?"

"It's just, this guy I dated said *he* could cook, too."

"So?" *What if she has a boyfriend?* He tried to ignore the shaft of jealousy as the thought occurred to him, but couldn't quite manage it. He could feel his teeth grinding. He would soon be an *ex* boyfriend if he and Kir had anything to say about it.

"So he set dinner down on the table."

"And?"

"And his cat tried to bury it."

Logan blinked, the tip of the pen arrested on the paper. "The cat what?"

"His cat hopped up onto the table, neat as you please, and tried to bury the food."

Logan tried to stifle the laugh, but knew he sounded strangled. "Was the cat right?"

"Hell, yes." He could hear the creak of her office chair as she leaned back. "A buzzard probably would have passed it by. The biscuits alone were prime building material."

Logan started to laugh.

"For some reason, he never called me back after that. Might have had something to do with me asking if he could make some more, since my mom really wanted to build this stone water feature out in her backyard."

Logan leaned back in his own chair, grinning like a loon. "Let me guess, they matched her siding or something?"

"Something like that. I got the impression I'd insulted him."

"Some guys have no sense of humor."

"Tell me about it."

***

Jordan bit back a moan as the last bite of tiramisu slipped between her lips. *He's gorgeous and he* cooks? *I'm in so much trouble.* "You, sir, can make me a meal anytime."

"I plan on it." Logan was smiling at her over the rim of his coffee cup. She felt her face heat up at the intensity of that smile. He'd been flirting with her off and on throughout the entire meal, and damn if she wasn't responding to his teasing touches and lingering glances.

Kir, on the other hand, had watched the two of them with indulgent amusement and a hint of heat, like a lazy cat basking in the sun, waiting his turn to play with the little mouse toy. And that's kind of how she felt. She was the small prey to their mighty hunters. The sad part was it was working. Her panties hadn't been this damp since her brother Magnus pushed her, fully dressed, into a lake when she was twelve.

Time to get things back on track before I leap across the table and do something foolish with my stupidly raging libido.

"Any ideas on what we should do for the video?" She turned to Kir, hoping to avoid Logan's lazy smile for a few moments. "What can you do that Logan can't do, other than thunderstorms?" She leaned forward, putting her chin on top of her folded hands, and stared at Kiran intently, her mind starting to drift into what she thought of as "work mode". "We need the video to prove to the others that it's really *you* and not some trick of Logan's."

Logan sat back and watched them quietly, his fingers casually cradling his coffee cup. Kiran nodded slowly. "One way would be to perform some kind of miracle." He exchanged a quick look with Logan, who shrugged. "There are differences between the magic of the Jotun and the miracles performed by the gods."

"What differences?"

"For instance, if it's associated with the spring season, I can influence it. Spring storms, flowering plants, green and growing things, are all under my influence."

"Don't forget sex and fertility."

Kir rolled his eyes, but not before she'd seen the quick heat come and go at the mention of sex. "Down, you horn-dog." He turned back to Jordan. "So, okay, add fertility to the list."

"Is there anything Logan can do that they'd point at and say, 'That's Loki, not Baldur'? In other words, can Logan imitate you?"

Logan's expression sobered immediately, the two men exchanging a long look. "That's been part of the problem for years. As a Trickster God, I *can* imitate quite a bit of what Kir can do, but if you know what to look for you can tell it's not the real deal."

Kir leaned forward and propped his chin on his hand with an irritated frown. "No matter what we do, Grimm can claim it was Loki and the others believe him. We need to come up with something that's indisputably Baldur." Kir sat back again with a sigh. "The problem is, what can I do that Logan can't imitate?"

"Hopefully the video itself will fix some of that."

Jordan looked at Logan. He was staring at her mouth. "Earth to Logan, come in, Logan."

His gaze snapped up, his mouth curling into that devil's grin she was coming to know so well. "If they can see *Baldur* performing the miracles, they'll know it's really him. There are some things I can imitate, but there are one or two things I simply can't imitate. Those are the ones we'll use."

She ignored him when his gaze went once more to her mouth. "*How* will they know it's you and not him?"

Kir looked…guilty. "They'll know."

She raised one brow in disbelief. "Just because they can see you?"

He nodded, looking uncomfortable.

"Are you going to share with the class?"

Kir ignored the question and began gathering the dishes.

Logan leaned forward, one finger stroking a line of fire down the back of her hand. "I'm more than willing to share." He glanced at Kir, who was now standing behind her chair, one strong hand resting on the table beside her plate. They had her surrounded in their heat. "Are you?"

Jordan gulped. *Good-bye dry panties, hello inner slut-puppy.*

The satisfaction on Logan's face as he stood to help her out of her seat didn't help. Kir's hand at the small of her back, guiding her out of the room as Logan took over clearing the table was almost a relief.

Almost. Kir's hand stroked her back in small, gentle circles as he guided her into the living room. It felt so good, she almost melted at his feet.

Oh, yes. So much trouble.

***

Kir watched as Jordan checked out the computer, making some notes on the programs they had. She was muttering to herself, Adobe this and Movie Maker that. Logan was sprawled on the sofa, watching her with that lazy, hooded look that always sent heat straight to Kir's cock.

She bent over to examine the plugs and slots on the laptop. The fabric of her jeans stretched taut across her shapely ass, displaying it perfectly. Kir nearly groaned out loud.

She couldn't have picked a more perfect way to torture them if she'd tried.

He heard Logan move on the sofa and knew he'd had the same reaction to the sight of Jordan bent over. He could picture one of them fucking her while the other watched, the two of them taking turns to make her scream. Better yet, one of them fucking her sweet, sweet pussy while the other reamed her tight ass, making her so tight she'd nearly squeeze their cocks off.

And none of the visuals currently running around in his head would get them any closer to their twin goals of winning their freedom and gaining their now ultimate prize: Jordan.

"So, what do you think?" He shifted in his seat as his erection throbbed against the zipper of his jeans. Damn, he wanted her.

Logan stood and moved over to the side of Kir's chair, his gaze never leaving the small woman moving around the laptop on the dinette table.

"I can work with this, not a problem. We need to pick up a camcorder, though, one that works with YouTube." She stood, hands on hips, her expression completely professional. The uncertain female they'd lazily seduced over dinner was gone, replaced by the confident, strong woman she'd first shown them in her office.

Kir wanted to take that woman and flip her onto her back, her legs over his shoulders as he... *Better not go there, or I'll have a permanent zipper mark on my cock.*

From the uncomfortable look on Logan's face it might already be too late for him.

"I know exactly where to pick one up, too. We'll head over there tomorrow."

"Why not use yours? Don't PIs all have camcorders?"

She grimaced. "I broke it last night. Or, should I say, I had it broken for me."

Kir's eyes narrowed. "Excuse me?" *Someone laid hands on her?* Thunder sounded off in the distance and he quickly averted his eyes. There were just some things he didn't think she was ready to see yet, the sharp edge of his temper being one of them.

She shrugged. "Not everyone appreciates having their cheating ways videotaped. Some of them get violent. Luckily I'd already removed the tape when she took the camera from me."

"She?" Kir's tension eased a bit. From the way Logan was standing, however, the revelation that Jordan's adversary had been female hadn't alleviated any of *his* anger.

"The other woman, in this case. The dickhead husband just stood there and laughed." She said the words absently, like what had happened was no big deal.

"Who was he?" Unless you knew Logan really well, you'd think the question was casual. Logan's expression was one Kir had seen before, and it did not bode well for whoever Jordan had been tailing. Considering he wasn't happy with the unknown man either, he was not inclined to enlighten her.

Jordan didn't know Logan well enough to figure out that he was supremely pissed off. "Just a bozo who doesn't know how to keep it zipped in his pants."

Logan's head tilted. "You know, if you tell me who it is, I can visit a little something special on him." Kir could see the fire dance in Logan's eyes, quickly doused by the other man's will.

Someone is in for an interesting time. He had no doubt that Logan would find out who the man was and make his life…interesting, whether she told them who it was or not. He relaxed, knowing the man and his mistress would pay for laying hands on their woman.

Wait. When was that decided?

She grinned. "Like what, an STD?"

"Nah. Odds are he'll get that anyway." Logan waved off Jordan's nod of agreement. "I mean something along the lines of dead fish in his curtain rods."

Jordan's grin melted away. "Huh?"

"Just tell your client that when she files for divorce she should let him have the curtains, complete with rods." His expression was devilish. "Trust me."

"I've heard of that before. Something about sewing dead prawns into the bottoms of the curtains, and when the fish rotted, the cheating couple was forced to move due to the smell. Only they took the curtains with them." She leaned against the dinette and crossed her arms over her chest. "That's some kind of urban legend, isn't it?"

Logan nodded. "And it makes a hell of a stench, too."

She stared at him. "Are you telling me it *isn't* an urban legend?"

"I am telling you no such thing."

Her expression of disbelief was almost as amusing as Logan's attempt at innocence. "Why don't I believe you?"

Logan chuckled as he took her arm and led her to the chaise. "Do we know now what we need to pick up tomorrow at the video store?"

Jordan was still frowning at him, but allowed him to lead her to the chaise. She seemed startled when Logan took a seat on the chaise next to her, draping his arm casually along the edge behind her. "Yes, I know exactly what we need tomorrow."

Her face was suspicious again. Kir took a seat on the ottoman across from her, his knees brushing hers. He did his best to look harmless, but he wasn't certain if he managed it or not.

"Good. Work's over, right?"

Kir saw the expression on Logan's face and knew he was about to make some sort of move on Jordan. "I think we're done for the evening, yes."

Jordan clapped her hands, making both Kir and Logan jump. He'd been lost in a vision of the two of them seducing her. "Good! Then I'll head home and meet you guys nice and early." She tried to stand, only to find

Logan's hand on her shoulder. The confusion on her face forced Kir to hide the smile threatening to get away from him.

"How about a movie?" Kir gave Jordan his best "I'm harmless, you can trust me" look.

"What movie?" From her expression she wasn't buying it. She still looked suspicious.

"What would you like to watch?"

"Your door shutting behind me as I head home for the night."

"I'm not sure we have that one."

Jordan rolled her eyes and got to her feet. "Seriously, if we're going to get to work in the morning, I need to head out." She looked down at her watch and groaned. "Damn, it's later than I thought."

"Then stay here for the night." Kir stood, checking out the clock on the entertainment center and grimaced. *Midnight. Not sure I want her driving home this late, especially if Grimm catches wind of us meeting.*

Jordan started hunting around for the small carry-on luggage she called a purse. "No, thanks. It's really late, and I need my sleep, something I don't think I'll get if I stay here."

"You got that right."

Kir kicked Logan's ankle as discreetly as he could, glad that Jordan's distraction kept her from hearing the other man's muttered words. "Then do us a favor?"

"What?"

"Let us walk you to your car, and call us once you're home."

"Why?"

"To make sure you get home safely."

She seemed to think about that for a moment before nodding. "All right."

Logan got out the door first, making sure it was safe before going to the elevator.

This left Kir to enjoy the view of the two best asses in the world walking right in front of him.

He was glad to see Jordan drove a sensible sedan, though it was an older model than he liked. Logan assisted her into her car, every inch the gentleman, shutting her door for her and watching carefully as she started her car.

She waved good-bye as she pulled out of the parking garage, confusion still lighting her features but a smile dragging at her lips.

Logan walked over to Kir, his arm going around Kir's waist and pulling him back to the elevator. Kir smiled. "That went well."

Logan snorted. "It didn't go *that* well. She's not upstairs."

Kir smiled. "Patience, love."

Logan pulled Kir into the elevator and pressed the button for their floor. "Patience is a virtue, and you know I'm not very virtuous."

"I noticed something you didn't."

"What?"

"Her scent."

The elevator began to rise, along with Logan's grin. "Ahh. Damp, was she?"

Kir looked over at his lover, not surprised to see that Logan's cock was a hard ridge behind his jeans.

Sometimes it paid to be a fertility god. It allowed you to notice all sorts of things others might wish you couldn't. "Very."

Logan took his hand, holding it against his thigh as they watched the numbers rise. His thumb absently stroked Kir's palm, soothing him. His smile was smug. "Good."

***

Logan watched the sassy sway of Jordan's ass as they got out of Kir's Mustang. They were headed to a computer store on Market Street Jordan frequented. She wanted to pick up a video camera with some sort of YouTube specific software, or hardware, or whatever. He wasn't quite sure what the hell that was supposed to mean, but he figured she did, and that was good enough for him. And Kir had nodded like he knew what she was talking about, so as far as he was concerned it was all good. The two of them had chattered like happy little techno-geeks the entire ride over while Logan amused himself by shooting imaginary bullets at every pigeon, blackbird and crow he could see.

Kir glanced back at Logan with a frown. "Are you sure this is going to work?"

Logan rolled his eyes. Kir was such a worrier sometimes. It drove him nuts. Kir and Jordan might have the technology down pat, but when it came to the magic part...that was the part where Logan shined. Kir should know better than to worry about *that* part.

"Yes," Jordan answered, confidence seeping from every pore as she stepped aside. Logan pushed her seat forward so he could get out of the Cracker-Jack box Kir called a car. "Follow me, boys."

"With pleasure," he purred.

She looked over her shoulder and rolled her eyes at him, but he could still see the uncertainty in her.

He noticed Kir's attention was also focused on Jordan's ass and stifled a smile. Since they'd decided to claim the luscious Jordan for their own neither one had kept their interest to themselves. Jordan was acting a little confused by all of the attention. She'd better get used to it. She was going to be on the receiving end of a *lot* of attention, if they had their way.

The thought of Kir, Jordan, chocolate sauce and tongue baths was probably what kept him from noticing the large blue sedan that pulled up alongside them.

Jordan bellowed "Down!" as she pushed him hard enough to knock him on his ass. It was his first clue that something was seriously wrong. A sound like a firecracker pierced the afternoon air. Jordan grunted in pain, and Logan literally saw red.

Kir landed on top of him, sandwiching Jordan between them. The blue sedan sped off, pedestrians shrieking and diving for cover. Kir rolled off him and immediately took Jordan into his arms. Logan stood, ready to chase down the blue sedan and have a little "chat" with the driver.

"Jordan!"

Something in Kir's deepened, panicked voice stopped him from chasing down the blue sedan. He looked at the woman cradled in Kir's arms, and his heart stopped. He knelt down beside Kir, instinctively placing himself between them and the street.

She'd been shot. Blood seeped from a wound in her right shoulder. Her eyes were glazed in pain as she looked up at him. Her features were determined as she grabbed a hold of Logan's shirt and pulled him close, hissing through clenched teeth, "He was aiming for *you*." Her eyes went to Kir. "Get him the fuck outta here."

And Logan slipped from being a little bit in love to being all the way. No one, *no one*, had ever taken pain meant for him. No one had *ever* gotten in between him and danger. No one had ever tried to protect him, or bled for him. No one had cared enough.

No one but Kir.

He saw the look on Kir's face, knew Kir felt the same damn way. That overprotective streak of Kir's was now fully engaged at the sight of the woman they'd claimed bleeding on the sidewalk. Kir was beyond furious as he cradled her to him, wincing in sympathy as she hissed.

An enraged Kir was a scary thing.

Kir stood, growling as Jordan gasped in pain, and ran for the car. He put her in the backseat, cursing the tiny sports car, while Logan dug in Kir's pocket for his keys.

"Jefferson's closest." Kir's voice had deepened. The pupils of his eyes turned white, storm clouds beginning to edge out the sunny blue. Logan reached into the glove compartment and handed Kir his mirrored shades, hiding his inhuman eyes from sight, then pulled on his own shades. Thunder sounded as grey clouds rapidly began to roll in over the city.

"Right." He waited long enough for Kir to close the passenger side door before taking off like a bat out of hell for Jefferson University Hospital.

They pulled up outside the emergency room entrance just as the rain started. Kir ran inside and managed to get a gurney for Jordan. It had taken a slight shift in the paperwork to get her seen first, but at this point he'd have been willing to blow on trumpets until she got taken care of, let alone a measly flexing of his powers. She was taken in, immediately assessed and moved straight into a curtained-off area, where a physician began prepping her for surgery.

"Excuse me; is either of you gentlemen related to the victim?"

Logan took his gaze off the curtains where Jordan was being prepped to look down at the nurse standing next to him. Her grey-streaked, no-nonsense bun was twisted, her brown eyes sympathetic as she clutched a clipboard to her chest.

"She's my wife."

He felt Kir start as the words slipped out of his mouth. He flexed his powers again to adjust all of Jordan's paperwork from *Grey* to *Saeter*. It wasn't enough to change her insurance and license; he'd changed *all* of her legal paperwork. The larger change took less energy and concentration. While he was at it he filed a marriage license with the state, just because…well, because. It soothed the beast inside him that needed to claim her firmly as his.

For a prankster god, it was a piece of cake.

The woman looked relieved. "I need you to sign the surgical release forms, please."

He signed everything she shoved at him, determined to see to it that his woman got the care she needed.

He looked over at Kir, who was staring at the curtained off area, a fierce frown covering his face. The thunder was louder now; the rain was coming down harder. The street was almost invisible out the window of the surgical waiting room.

Make that our *woman.* Lightning arced across the sky, confirming his thought.

He stood there, clenching and unclenching his hands as he heard the doctor give the order to have Jordan wheeled to surgery. He was having a hard time controlling the raging fires within him. Someone, some *stranger*, was going to be cutting into her flesh, removing a bullet meant for him, and it was driving him crazy. The knowledge that he could have lost someone else he loved burned like acid in his gut. Memory flashed behind his eyes of his sons, Nari and Narfi, one dead by the other's hand. Nari lost to madness for all time as he killed his brother; Narfi's entrails enchanted to hold down a god and used to bind Loki to the mountain.

Strong arms wrapped around him and held tight while inside he raged against the memories, both past and present.

"How come she gets to be *your* wife?" Kir grumbled.

Logan felt some of his anger drain away as Kir stroked his back.

"She could be *my* wife, you know." He felt Kir grin briefly against his neck, but it didn't fool him. Kir was shaking. The urge to soothe his lover began to overtake the rage and pain inside him. "After all, she likes me better."

Kir sounded like a petulant child, but Logan knew the truth. Blondie was just as upset, and just as furious, as he was. Logan snorted. Shaking his head, he wrapped his arms around Kir, and settled down to wait for the doctors to return.

***

Jordan woke to nausea and confusion. She blinked, looking up at the bright white light overhead. "Don't go into the light," she muttered, surprised when someone snorted next to her. *Logan.* Her brain immediately identified the sound, like she'd heard it hundreds of times before. *Of course, I* have *damn near heard it a hundred times before.*

She turned her head, surprised at how difficult it was. Her stomach rolled with nausea. She swallowed hard, fighting back the urge to hurl all over Logan's expensive leather jacket. He looked pissed as all hell. "Where's Kir?"

"Right here." She felt someone take hold of her hand. "Told you she likes me better." Soft lips brushed her forehead. She turned to see Kir smiling down at her, concern shadowing his eyes. "Hi."

"Hi."

Another pair of soft lips brushed her forehead. "Welcome back."

She looked up into Logan's face, surprised at his fierce expression. "Thanks. Where'd I go?"

"You got shot." She felt his hand tremble in hers, and tried to squeeze it, surprised at both the emotion flooding his face and how hard it was to get her hand to work. "Don't you *ever* put yourself between me and a bullet again, you hear me?"

She closed her eyes wearily and licked her lips. "Yup. Next time, let your ass get shot. Got it."

"Jordan."

Her eyes opened to see Logan frowning down at her.

"Shh. Not now, Logan." The two men exchanged a look over her head. She would have tried to figure out what it meant, but she was so damn tired. "Go to sleep, sweetheart. We'll be back soon to take you home." Before she could process the fact that Kir had called her sweetheart, he gave her the sweetest kiss she'd ever received.

"He's right. Get some rest." Logan's mouth replaced Kir's. His kiss was full of carefully banked fire. "We'll be back in about an hour."

She had a hard time keeping her eyes open after the two men left her room, talking quietly as the door shut behind them. *What the hell was that all about?* She drifted off to sleep, wondering what it would be like to have the two of them *really* kissing her.

***

"What do you mean, you missed?"

Val winced at the hissed words as his father turned to face him. "I hit Jordan."

"What the *fuck* was Jordan doing there?"

"I believe they may have hired her."

Grimm's mouth tightened. Val made sure to keep all expression from his face as Grimm glared at him. "So what stopped you from finishing the job?"

Val blinked. "I shot Jordan."

"And?"

Val didn't answer, knowing there was no point.

"If Jordan is helping them, you need to remove her, as well. *No excuses.*"

He bowed his head to his father, hoping the man didn't see the hatred in his eyes. The reason for his birth, the vengeance against his brother's murderer and the punishment of the man who'd masterminded it, had instead become service to the betrayer and an unending hunt for the betrayed.

And it was seriously beginning to piss him off, especially now that the end was so tantalizingly near. But the end had been near before, and Grimm had managed to stave it off.

He kept his expression blank as he left the office, knowing that his time was running out. If Jordan was working with Loki and Baldur, Tyr would soon find out. And Grimm would no longer accept mistakes.

How did the idiot miss again?

Grimm ground his teeth together, fighting down the urge to throw something. Something glass, that would make a nice, loud, shattering noise as it hit. He eyed the glass apple his wife Frederica had given him for Christmas about forty-five years ago and seriously thought about it. *Better not. She'll notice the next time she's in the office and question it. Stupid bitch.*

And the only person he couldn't afford questions from was Frigg. Her visions had let her know some of what he'd planned for Baldur and Hodr, but not all.

Not enough to stop him completely.

If Loki hadn't interfered, things would have worked out a great deal differently. And now Jordan, the traitorous little bitch, was picking Loki's side over his. And if Loki stayed true to form, there was no *way* Val was getting anywhere near Jordan or Baldur again.

Unless…

Grimm smiled, and the window in front of him frosted over.

"Well. I see you're having happy thoughts."

Grimm turned to see Rina Southerland, Val's mother, standing in the doorway to his office. "Rina."

She shut the door behind her and smiled seductively. "We have a date tonight, remember?"

He smiled again. Indulging Rina was one of his favorite pastimes. And since Frederica was at one of her charity functions, he had more than enough time to indulge himself, as well. "Of course. How could I forget?" He walked over and pulled her roughly to him, kissing her passionately as she cupped his thickening cock through his slacks. For her he changed into the virile young man he truly was, not the Old Grimm everyone thought him to be.

For a frost-Jotun, Rina had more fire in her than any other woman he'd ever bedded, including his wife. And, buried balls-deep in her pale, slender body, he even managed to forget his troubles for a little while.

Too bad he was going to have to kill her before he killed Val. After all, a wise man knew better than to rouse a mother bear.

***

Kir watched carefully as Logan placed Jordan in the back seat of his Lexus. They'd opted to buy the car when they realized how uncomfortable Jordan would be in Kir's Mustang. Logan had insisted on one of the best, most luxurious SUVs on the market and, since it would be Logan's car, Kir hadn't objected too much.

The trip back to their penthouse was surprisingly uneventful. The ride in the luxury SUV was smooth and quiet. Jordan dozed, not surprising considering the amount of blood she'd lost and the strength of the painkillers she was on.

He'd warned her that Val wouldn't hesitate to kill her if Grimm ordered it. He'd been half hoping he was wrong, but once again his father and brother had proven to him how little innocent lives mattered to them.

It had taken every bit of Logan's power to keep her family from finding her. One wrong move and Grimm would have been breathing down their necks. As it was, Kir knew they were probably going to have some pissed off younger Grimms on their doorstep soon. Jordan was begging them to call her siblings and he and Logan were close to giving in, at least where Jeff and her sister Jamie were concerned. No way in hell were they going to call Magnus and Morgan Grimm. And they couldn't tell her of the phone calls they were receiving from her sister. Some of them had made Kir's hair stand on end. They'd started out pleasant enough, but the last one had been filled with threats that he was pretty sure were anatomically impossible without the aid of kitchen utensils and a lot of Vaseline. He still had no idea what a "rotating pineapple attachment" was, but he was pretty sure he didn't want to find out.

"She'll be all right."

He looked over at Logan, whose eyes never left the road. "I know."

"Are you really pissed that I put my name on the paperwork?"

Kir smiled. Logan was frowning, the expression one that let Kir know he was prepared to fight for his way. "No, just so long as she understands she's committed to both of us."

Logan snorted. "Once we've got her naked between us, she'll figure it out pretty damn quick."

A muffled snore sounded from the backseat. Kir turned to see Jordan's face buried in the upholstery. She'd been in the hospital for almost a week and was still exhausted. Logan had put wards around her bed to keep her safe, but even then it had been a harrowing time. He couldn't keep *everyone* from touching her.

"How do we keep this from happening again?"

Kir bit his lip. "I don't know."

"Her fathers are going to pitch a fit when they find out what happened."

"Not to mention her boss. And her brothers and sister."

They looked at each other and winced. "Can we prove it was Val that shot her?"

Kir shook his head. "And even if we could, they'd still blame us for putting her in danger."

"Not us. Me."

Kir didn't say anything as Logan pulled into the parking garage and shut off the engine. They'd have to make sure the Lexus was added to their parking allotment, or they'd get towed. Since they didn't use their powers any more than necessary that meant a long, boring trip to the manager's office and filling out paperwork. Kir picked up Jordan, much to Logan's disgust. He smirked at Logan's disgruntled frown. "Your car, your paperwork."

Logan groaned at Kir's grin. "Great. Where's an assassin or two when you need one?"

**

Logan left the manager's office with a smirk on his face. He'd gotten a lecture from the overly fussy man on informing management about any "changes to the status of the tenancy of the condo". Logan had been tempted to go back as the owner and give the man hell for upsetting a rich client, but he didn't really have time for that sort of fun. So he'd chosen a different form of punishment for the pompous asshole. He grinned. He wondered how long it would take before the manager noticed that his signature on every single document in that office had been changed to Dick Head.

He snickered as he stepped into the elevator. Kir would probably shake his head and try to talk him into changing it back. Jordan seemed more the type to try and *make* him change it back. And maybe he would change *most* of it back.

Maybe. If they begged really prettily.

He headed up to the twenty-second floor, eager to see them both, hoping Kir had settled her down in *their* bedroom. The thought of Jordan's scent mingling with his and Kir's on their sheets was irresistible.

He opened the door to find Kir scowling at Jordan, who was busy trying to set up the video camera one-handed. She was pale and shaking.

Logan glared at her, all of his instincts screaming at him that she needs to be resting, not fucking around with electronics. And since his instincts were backed up by her doctor's orders, he felt fully justified in growling at her. "What the fuck do you think you're doing?"

She looked up at him and smiled wearily. "We need to get the YouTube video going."

"Now?"

"The sooner the better."

"The doctor said you're supposed to be in bed." He turned to Kir. "Why isn't she in bed?"

"Because when I went to pick her up she started struggling and I was afraid she'd reopen the wound."

Thunder sounded outside, letting Logan know exactly how upset Kir was. The fact that Kir hadn't taken his eyes off Jordan was also not a good sign. He looked out the window to see a fine spring shower raining down on the city. "To bed, Jordan."

She stood up with a wince, her face paling even more. Beads of sweat dotted her forehead. "No."

Logan gritted his teeth. "I think Kir and I can figure out how to take a fucking video. Go. To. *Bed.*"

She put one hand on her hip, the other half in and half out of the sling the doctor wanted her to wear. "When I'm done." She glared at him. "Oh, and by the way, I'm *still* not sure why you guys brought me here instead of to my apartment, other than the fact that you think Uncle Val will come after me there." She turned back to the equipment, muttering to herself.

When she hissed in pain, Logan decided enough was enough.

He looked at Kir, who nodded. Together the two men moved on Jordan, Kir in the back, Logan in front. They sandwiched her between them before she knew what they were doing.

"Guys, this isn't funny—*hey!*"

Kir held her arms while Logan picked her up. Together they two-stepped her into the bedroom. Ignoring her protests, Logan kicked the door shut behind him. The two men carefully put Jordan down on the bed.

Logan stood and pointed a finger at her. "Stay."

"Woof."

He narrowed his eyes. "I mean it."

"Yes, Daddy."

He raked his eyes up and down her figure, allowing her to see the heat in his eyes. "Set one pinky toe off that bed, and *Daddy* will give you the spanking you deserve. Got it?" He grinned. "And don't think *Mommy* will stop me, either."

"Asshole," Kir muttered. He handed Jordan a glass of water and a pain pill. "Here. Don't worry about the video. Logan and I will take care of it."

She made a face at them, popped the pill, and settled back down against the pillows. She looked like a pissed-off kid who'd been told to take a nap. "Do you have any idea what you're going to do for the video?"

The look on Kir's face reminded Logan of a naughty little boy. "I have an idea or two."

***

Jordan stared at the two men blearily and wondered what they were up to. They'd exchanged a long look over her body before Kir pulled the comforter over her, careful of her shoulder. "An idea or two. Why am I not reassured?" She yawned as the pain pill began working on her.

"Don't you trust us?"

Two identical, angelic looks, neither of which she trusted. "Hell, no."

Logan started to laugh. "Smart girl."

Kir just shook his head. "Get some rest, and let us worry about the video, okay?" He leaned down and gave her a kiss. She tried to stop him, hissing in pain when she tried to move her bad arm. Kir stopped her, gently pressing her arm back down. "Don't do that."

Logan leaned over her, taking Kir's place. "Aren't you the one who said you don't like pain?"

She stuck out her tongue and blew a raspberry at him.

He kissed her quickly, before she could pull her tongue back in.

"What is up with all of the sudden sucking of face?" She was yawning before she even completed the sentence.

Logan turned and sauntered out of the bedroom. "I'll wake you in time for dinner, sweetheart."

Sweetheart? She turned to Kir, who was smiling down at her. He was wavering in and out of focus. "Kir?"

He brushed her hair away from her forehead. "It's simple. We've decided to keep you."

She blinked up at him sleepily. *Damn, those pain pills are good.* She watched him walk out of the bedroom door, gently shutting it behind him. *I could have sworn he just said they're keeping me...*

She drifted off to sleep before she could finish the thought.

***

Kir waited until he knew for certain Jordan was asleep. "Got the camera?"

"Yup." Logan hefted the bag. They'd quietly dismantled all of the equipment, trying their best not to disturb Jordan. Kir's idea was a great one, but they had to head into Rittenhouse Square to make it work. Luckily he'd calmed down enough for the rain to stop, or they would have had to wait since the camera wasn't waterproof.

Logan set up the wards while Kir made sure everything was locked up tight. Logan had had to adjust them due to Jordan's presence, but the extra step hadn't seemed to faze him at all. "All set."

They headed for the elevator and made their way outside. They walked quickly to a secluded part of the park, shivering in the early spring air. They ducked behind the statue "Lion Crushing a Serpent," by the French sculptor Antoine-Louis Barye; the area was small and surrounded by bushes on three sides, perfect for what they wanted to do. At this time of night the kids who liked to climb the lion were already home, safely tucked away in bed. Logan set up the camera while Kir prepared the pot of soil he'd brought with him.

Kir took a deep, calming breath, and let it out slowly. "Ready when you are."

Logan's warm smile helped ease his jitters. *Here goes nothing.*

Chapter Five

"Hello?"

"He's alive, Oliver."

Grimm blinked, the blood rushing to his head as his temples throbbed. "Frederica, what are you talking about?"

"Our son, Oliver. Baldur is *alive*."

He sighed, trying his best to sound weary while his mind scrambled on how she could know the truth after all this time. "Darling, you know he's not. Hermod himself confirmed it when he saw Baldur in the Underworld." And wasn't it a relief that Hermod was as stupid as he was gullible, or he would have noticed that Baldur was *breathing*.

Hermod was also known to be honest to a fault. He'd seen Baldur in Hel; therefore, Baldur must be dead, reinforcing the lie he'd told.

Good old Hermod. Grimm wondered if he was enjoying the Underworld as much as Hodr was.

"Have you had your tonic today, sweetheart?"

She paused, her breathing harsh over the phone. "No."

The extra-strength potion he'd made for her to take while Baldur and Loki were so close to his home territory would take the edge off her nosiness. "Take some, before you make yourself ill over this travesty of a hoax. I'll deal with Loki myself. I promise you that."

She paused again, then meekly said, "All right."

He heard her sipping and smiled. *Stupid cow.* Keeping her docile had been remarkably easy once he figured out the secret of the apples. "Now, go rest, and allow me to deal with Loki's treachery."

"I've sent you the link to the video he made, Oliver." He could hear her stifling tears. "It looks so much like our Baldur, right down to the eyes."

Grimm's blood ran cold at the thought. "I'll take a look, my dear. Go rest."

She sniffed. "Will you be home tonight?"

He thought of Rina, and the silken present she'd promised him that night. "No, dear, I think I'd better take care of this problem as soon as possible. Don't you think?"

She sighed. "Of course."

In his most loving, caring voice, Grimm said, "Get some rest. I love you." He practically gagged on the words.

"I love you too."

He hung up, and opened the email Frigg had sent him.

By the end of the video, his entire office was covered in frost.

***

Val clicked open the email link his father had sent him. *Deal with this!* had been the subject line. Val had no idea what had the Old Man's briefs in a bunch this time…

His jaw dropped open in shock as Baldur's face took up his screen. He clicked on the "play" button.

"Hello, Aesir and Vanir." Baldur's beautiful voice purred in Old Norse. Those pale eyes were cold as ice. "I think you all know who I am. Or maybe not." Baldur moved back, smiling gently as he did so. Val shivered. "After all, you've been trying to kill me for centuries now, haven't you? Quite frankly, I'm getting tired of it."

The sudden deepening of his voice had Val leaning forward in his chair. *What are they up to?*

"Ever since that day in the Thing, you have hunted us and hounded us. You have given us no peace. You have murdered wives and sons, turned brother against brother, and destroyed lives in your quest to destroy my lover. But enough is enough. I will tolerate no more.

"A week ago Jordan Grey was shot trying to protect Loki and me." He leaned in close to the camera again. Val groaned when he saw that Baldur's pupils had started to turn white. *That's bad.* "By the way, Val, I owe you one for that." He pulled back to the sound of a dark chuckle. *Loki's there. Make that* very *bad.* "I owe *all* of you, actually." His eyes left the camera lens long enough to watch Loki walk around and take position behind Baldur. "Watch carefully, people. I'm only going to do this once." Baldur stared into the camera, his gentle smile never wavering, as the pot he'd been holding quivered. A sprig of green appeared, rapidly growing in Baldur's hands until a perfectly formed white lily opened its trumpet-like flower. Behind him, all of the bushes sprouted tiny flowers as well, blue with white centers, just like Baldur's eyes.

It was a miracle, since those bushes were obviously yews, and incapable of flowering. This meant that it really *was* Baldur standing there, and not some imposter like Grimm had been telling the gods for centuries. The magic of the Jotun, even Loki's, couldn't fake a *true* miracle.

"These flowers have bloomed to mark both an end and a beginning." Baldur's blue and white gaze was glued to the camera. Val couldn't shake the feeling that he was staring right at him. You barely noticed Loki standing behind him, somehow in shadow.

Val groaned. Baldur was glowing. It was *his* shadow his lover stood in.

"You all forgot something, you know. I am a God of Spring. I bring peace, hope, joy, et cetera." He waved his hand, careful not to knock over the lily. Val could hear Loki's snort of amusement behind Baldur, noted the first hint of warmth to enter those cold eyes. "Just as you have given me no peace, now I give you no peace." Those sky blue eyes darkened until the white pupils glared out of a circle of navy. "No gardens shall bloom, no sun shall shine for you. Winter is in your hearts to stay until justice is served, both for the torment you've given Loki and myself and the injuries you've done to our families."

At that point, Loki leaned forward, placing one hand on Baldur's shoulder. "By the way, Frey? Thor? Jordan's fine. We're keeping her safe." That devil's grin that had gotten him into so much trouble over the centuries was on his face. "And we've decided to just plain keep her."

Oh, shit. Val watched as the familiar YouTube scrolling screen appeared, asking people to rate the video. *Fuck, fuck, fuck.*

No wonder Grimm was ready to blow a gasket.

Frey and Thor would probably start bellowing like bulls, knowing that Jordan was in Loki's hands. It wouldn't matter to them that she was also in Baldur's hands, since they probably still believed Baldur was an imposter. He wondered how many phone calls Grimm had already gotten from them.

And he wondered how Frigg would take the news that her son was still alive.

He blinked, startled, as his hands left the keyboard. He'd just emailed the link to each and every one of the Aesir and Vanir in his address book.

Damn it, Loki! What the hell do you think you're doing?

But deep down, he knew. He just hoped Jordan didn't get any more hurt than she'd already been. If she hadn't leapt to Logan's defense, she never would have gotten hurt in the first place. He'd aimed the shot to miss by just a hair, a hair Jordan had stepped into. *Damn it.*

There was a gasp from outside his office. Stepping out to see what was going on, he saw plants withering and dying. And from the gasps and yelling he could hear, all of the plants in Grimm and Sons were doing the same.

The true meaning of Baldur's curse hit home.

He turned and went back into his office, trying to hide his snicker behind a cough.

Damn, bro. Way to make your point.

God of Spring, indeed.

***

The incessant pounding on the door had Logan groggily getting to his feet. Kir was sleeping in the bed with Jordan, making sure she didn't need anything, while Logan had stayed up all night working. He'd just fallen asleep on the sofa after a long bout of research, both on the computer and in some of the more esoteric books he owned.

It had been two days since they'd brought Jordan home, with orders to see to it that she got physical therapy. If Logan was right, though, she wouldn't need it.

He opened the door to a small, pissed-off redhead. Her wild curls danced around her head in their own fiery halo. Her foot was tapping a staccato beat as she glared at him. "Where's Jordan?"

"Good morning to you too, Jamie." He blinked sleepily, scratching at his naked chest as he yawned. It was too damn early in the morning for this. "Jordan's sleeping."

Her pixie eyes narrowed. "*Where?*"

He couldn't help it. He leered down at her. "In my bed. With Goldilocks."

She took a deep breath. "*Jordan!*"

He winced and fought the urge to cover his ears. She had a set of lungs on her that would make an opera singer proud. "Fuck, shut the hell up. You want to wake the whole damn floor?" He grabbed her by the arm and yanked her through, ignoring her gasp when the wards flared up around her. Something about that bothered him, but he was too damn tired to figure it out. "Jordan was shot. She's just out of the hospital and needs her rest."

She growled up at him, cute as a kitten. "Exactly. Moron. Which is why I'm here."

"What's up?" Kir stepped out of the bedroom, all rumpled and warm, his black sleep pants full of wrinkles. Logan wanted to just slurp him up, especially when he yawned and rubbed his six-pack abs.

Jamie growled again.

He pointed with his thumb at Jamie. "The Chihuahua here wants to know where Jordan is. Ow." He leaned over and rubbed his shin, glaring at Jamie. She'd actually kicked him, and now stood there, glowering at him. "Down, tiger."

"*Where is my sister?*" Jamie was actually shrieking, stamping her foot, her face turning beet red.

Kir looked at Logan and grimaced. "She's in bed, sleeping."

"Not anymore." A sleepy, grumpy-looking Jordan stuck her head out of the doorway. "Morning, Jamie. I see you haven't had your coffee yet."

"Jordan? You okay? Tweedledum here didn't want to let me in."

"I opened the damn door, didn't I?" He limped into the room, ignoring Kir's rolling eyes, and headed right for Jordan. He kissed her on top of her sleep-rumpled head. Her hair was sticking up, and it tickled his nose. He pouted down at her. "She kicked me."

"Poor baby." She patted him on the head, yawning again. "Go make coffee, will you?"

"Work, work, work." Logan paused by Kir long enough to exchange a quick kiss before he headed into the kitchen, grumbling.

"Cinderfelly, Cinderfelly, night and day it's Cinderfelly," Jordan sang as she headed back into the bedroom, presumably to get dressed.

Logan stopped, stunned. He put his hands on his hips and turned, not surprised to see Kir collapsed against the doorframe, laughing his ass off. "Very funny, dickhead. Why don't you go deal with the evil stepsister while I put coffee on, okay?"

He caught the look of suspicion on Jamie's face as he headed into the kitchen, but at least some of the anger had left her eyes. *Good. I don't want Jordan upset.* And having her baby sister fussing would upset her, big time.

Calling Jamie hadn't been in their plans, but Jordan had begged and pleaded for them to call her family. So they'd called Jeff, figuring he'd be the calmer of the twins. Poor Jeff had been stunned to hear what had happened, but he was out of town on a case and couldn't get back very quickly. He'd offered to call his brothers, Magnus and Morgan, but Kir had talked him out of it, saying Jordan wanted to talk to them herself. He just hoped little brother had listened, or he'd wind up with two pissed-off gods on his doorstep. Dealing with the twin, full-blooded sons of Thor was *not* on his to-do list today, thank you very much.

Apparently Jeff had opted to call little sis instead, who'd decided it was a *good* idea to show up at the ass-crack of dawn.

Wait. Two women, one of them pissed off, together in our condo. Neither one of whom has had caffeine.

He shuddered and did the only sane thing he could. He hid in the kitchen and made coffee.

***

Kir pulled away from the doorjamb and wiped the tears from his eyes. Little Jamie was still standing there, hands on hips, glaring at him like he'd run over her puppy.

"What?"

He was baffled when she shook her head at him like he was a loon. "How bad is she?" She plopped down on the white chaise, staring at him a little less angrily.

"Hurting." He winced when she glared at him again. "We're taking care of her, I promise."

"You don't even know her. How can you take care of her?"

He glided over to her, watching her face as she slowly took in his naked chest. The look was assessing and without heat.

The little minx is sizing me up!

"How does Jordan feel about this whole...arrangement?" She waved her hand in the air, her brows still furrowed. "I mean, she's pretty big on the whole monogamy thing."

"Tri-ogomy."

Jamie blinked. "Huh?"

Kir shrugged, and yawned again. It was too fuck-all early in the morning for her to try and get him to make sense. "Three people, all together. Not sure monogamy is the right word."

"So you two are going to sleep around on her?"

"Around her, on her, in her...yup, that covers it." He fell onto the sofa and put his arm over his eyes. Damn he was tired. Despite the fact that Jordan had slept most of the night peacefully next to him, it hadn't felt quite right. He'd missed having Logan in the bed with them. That would have made it perfect. But they'd been too afraid of jarring her healing shoulder to risk it.

"Pervert."

He sighed. "I love Jordan. I love Logan. Logan loves me. I'm working on Jordan. If that makes me a pervert, then hand me the flag and teach me the anthem."

"Kir?"

Jordan's hesitant voice had him sitting up. "Yes, baby?"

She held up one arm of the shirt she'd been trying to put on. She held her injured arm, in its sling, over her breasts. She'd managed to get the bra on, but not hooked.

He got up and, without thought, helped her finish dressing. "Better?"

"Mm-hmm. Thanks." Her cheeks were flushed and she wouldn't meet his eyes. She'd been like this since the first time he'd had to help her get dressed. Having a bullet wound sucked big time. Luckily it had been on the outside of her arm, rather than further in; the bones had been nicked, but not broken.

"You're welcome." He planted a soft kiss on those oh-so-tempting lips and left for the bedroom. If he was going to be up, he was going to take a shower. Maybe it would help wake him up.

Normally he would have dragged Logan in with him, but he didn't for two reasons. One, he was pretty sure Jamie would be weirded all the hell out. And two, they'd decided not to do anything with each other until *after* they'd convinced Jordan she belonged with them. Even if it led to a terminal case of blue balls.

Oh, well. Thank goodness for body wash and a firm grip. He grinned and shut the bathroom door behind him with an audible *click*. It didn't occur to him until he had the water nice and hot and was about to step in that her sister had been sitting right there, yet Jordan had still asked *him* for help.

Suddenly the day was looking a whole lot brighter.

***

Jordan sat on the sofa, sipping at the coffee Logan had brought out for her. It was perfect, just like everything the two men had done for her so far was perfect.

Make that almost perfect.

They had hovered over her for the last week, and for the most part, she was grateful for it, especially when she'd been stuck in the hospital for longer than they'd thought she would be. And when they'd brought her home two days ago she'd needed so much help that it hadn't even been funny. She couldn't quite dress herself, let alone feed herself. Having the two men pamper her was a heady feeling she could quickly grow addicted to, along with the tiny little touches and kisses they peppered her with. It was like they were slowly seducing her, since none of those little kisses they constantly gave her could be called "brotherly".

On the flip side, she could live without their bossiness. The one time yesterday she'd tried to sneak into the den to check her email, they'd freaked out and put her to bed like a recalcitrant four-year-old.

Of course, she could admit, at least to herself, that she'd *acted* like a recalcitrant four-year-old. She had the feeling today wasn't going to be much better.

"Y'know, you've got two. Can I have one? Because it's no fair hoarding the hotties."

Jordan smirked at Jamie over the rim of her mug. "What do you think Travis would have to say about that?"

Jamie turned beet red. "Absolutely nothing, since he doesn't know I exist outside of *Hi, this is Guardian Investigations. How may we help you?*" It was her best, perkiest receptionists' voice, the one that grated on Jordan's nerves until her third cup of coffee. "What do you think he's going to say when he finds out you've been shot? Hmm?"

Jordan leaned in and whispered, ignoring the twinge of pain in her shoulder. "I've already emailed him."

Jamie nodded, some of the flush receding from her cheeks. "Good. He needs to know, so we can fuss over you." She jumped. "All of us. I mean, all of us. Jeff, too. You know how he likes to fuss."

Jordan bit her lip. Jamie's crush on their boss never failed to lift her day. Too bad Travis had never shown any interest in her. The two of them would be smokin' hot together. "I can't lay claim to either Demon Boy *or* Archangel."

She thought she heard a muffled *bullshit* from the kitchen, but she wasn't certain. Could have been Logan sneezing. She shrugged and dismissed it.

One of Jamie's bright red brows rose into her hair. "Really? Because it looked to me like you and Mr.'s DB and AA are having a nice, cosy live-in. Complete with rumpled bedhead and delivered coffee."

"Line of duty. They feel guilty." Or, that's what she kept telling herself, anyway. "They're worried that the person who shot at them will go after me, and they have better security in their home than I do in mine." Which was the truth. A brain-dead monkey could probably break into her inexpensive apartment with ease.

Another muffled sound came from the kitchen. *Huh. Who knew? Gods sneeze. Logan needs to get his allergies checked.* She ignored the little voice that told her that what she'd heard had *not* been a sneeze.

"Really," Jamie drawled. She perked up, smiling that sunny smile that had landed her the receptionists' job at Guardian. "Y'know, with Travis away on vacation, I bet he wouldn't mind if you stayed at his place. The security there is top-notch."

She opened her mouth to answer when a hand landed on her good shoulder. "She's perfectly happy right here."

Jamie glared up at Logan. "*She's* capable of speech, ape."

Jordan nearly snorted coffee through her nose trying not to laugh.

Before she could regain her composure Kir stepped out of the bedroom. His cheeks were flushed, his hair hanging wet around his shoulders. He'd put on a muscle shirt, blue to match his eyes, and one of his sinfully tight pairs of jeans. His big feet were bare, braced squarely on the maple floor. A breezy smile graced his face. "I'm starving. Anybody want donuts?"

***

Logan stared down at Jordan's sleeping form. He still couldn't get over the fact that she'd bled for him. Not even Sigyn, who'd claimed to love him and left him when he'd fallen for Kir, had ever bled for him. And Kir *couldn't* bleed for him, though he'd thrown himself in front of Logan more than once in their long lives.

He never wanted her life endangered ever again. The very thought sent twin snakes of fear down his spine, and was the reason he'd barely slept in the last eight days.

His eyes narrowed as the blade cut into the palm of his hand. Blood bonding with Odin had given the god the power to shift his shape; maybe bonding with Jordan would give her the fast healing Logan enjoyed.

He cut her palm quickly, ignoring her hiss of pain as he slapped their hands together. He closed his eyes and focused on their joined wounds.

"What the hell?"

Jordan's sleepy, angry voice couldn't drown out the pounding of their hearts in his ears. He willed the blood to mingle, hers to him and his to her, each flowing into the other's veins.

Her gasp echoed his as their blood merged for all time.

"Ow, dickhead! What did you do that for?"

He opened his eyes and turned her hand over, eagerly checking to see if the wound had started closing.

It hadn't. *Fuck. So much for research.* His own wound was slowly closing before his eyes. "Shit."

"Wow. How are you doing that?"

"Logan?"

Logan turned to see Kir peering over his shoulder at their bloody hands. "It didn't work."

"What didn't work?" Jordan was looking back and forth between them, obviously confused.

"I was trying to speed up your healing."

She looked down at the bloody cut on her hand. "You're right. It didn't work."

"I'll get the medical kit." Kir headed into the bathroom.

"I'm sorry." Logan brushed his clean hand through her hair. "I was really hoping this would fix things."

Her face softened. "You meant well. I think."

He sighed. "When I became Odin's blood brother, he gained my ability to shift shape. I gained his immortality. I was hoping the bond would grant you my ability to heal quickly."

"Would that work on a human?"

He smiled. "You're not human, remember?"

"*Half* human, then." She looked down again at her hand, concerned. "If I didn't get healing, what *did* I get?"

He shrugged. As far as he was concerned she was welcome to all of his powers. "We'll have to wait and see."

Kir returned with the first-aid kit. "Give me your hand." He checked her cut, cleansing it with a washcloth. "It looks clean, and I don't think you need stitches." He bandaged it quickly, pressing a kiss to her knuckles when he was done. "All better."

"Thanks, Mom."

His expression turned wicked. Logan knew that look, and felt his cock harden in his jeans. It was the look Kir used when he was in the mood to play.

"Any other boo-boos you'd like me to kiss?"

Logan grinned as Kir waggled his eyebrows outrageously.

As Jordan giggled, he leaned over and brushed his lips over Kir's. *Time to see if she can handle the three of us together.* "I have a boo-boo you can kiss."

"Ugh. Get a room, guys. Some of us are trying to sleep."

He looked down to see embarrassment written all over her bright red face. She'd screwed her eyes shut tightly, but the curve of her lips let him know she was amused. *No disgust; that's good. And is that…? Yes! Ah, the sight of an aroused woman.* Her nipples were perky, pushing up against the fabric of her top.

"Tell you what. I'll kiss your boo-boo and Kir can kiss mine."

When her eyes popped open his lips were already on hers. He stroked his tongue against her closed lips, silently asking her to let him in. *Please, let me in.* He was dying for a taste of her.

Kir's mouth began a slow exploration of his neck, his hands pulling the shirt from Logan's jeans. He lifted from the kiss long enough for Kir to finish pulling the shirt from his body.

"Guys?"

"Hmm?" Logan leaned down and licked a line from her neck to her chin. Her shiver filled him with the need to see what else he could do to make her quiver like that.

Kir's fingers reached around Logan and began tugging on Jordan's shirt buttons.

Good idea. Logan began helping him, ignoring Jordan's feeble attempts to bat their hands away.

"Guys!"

"What?"

Kir sounded as distracted as he was. They were both busy staring at Jordan's exposed breasts. They gave identical happy sighs. *Mmm...no bra.* Rosy, hard nipples were exposed to their delighted gazes.

"No."

Logan blinked. *No?*

"No?" Kir sounded shocked.

"*No.*"

Logan stared at Kir. "She said no."

"Shit." Kir looked back down at Jordan. "Why?"

"What do you mean, why?" She pulled her shirt closed, holding the pieces together with one hand.

Logan's frown was fierce. "We want you. You want us. We plan on keeping you. *I blood bonded you.* So, yeah. Why no?"

"More importantly, why yes?" Jordan stared at both of them, her brows drawn down in a frown.

It was Logan's turn to be shocked. "Why *yes*?" Hadn't they done everything in their power to show her how they felt over the last week? Just dealing with her pint-sized, psychopathic sister should have gotten them brownie points galore!

She sighed. "You two are a couple. You've been together for so long I can't even begin to imagine it. Why on earth would you bring someone else into your bed? Unless you do this kind of thing all the time?" Her frown had become ferocious. Logan could easily read the jealousy she was trying to hide.

Apparently they hadn't proven to her how they felt. "No!"

"Uh-uh. Don't be absurd." Kir sat up, looking offended. "I haven't slept with anyone other than Logan since that day at the Thing!"

"Ditto. Other than trading 'Logan' for 'Kir', that is."

Her jaw worked as the jealousy was replaced by confusion. "Then why would you put me into bed with you two?"

Logan and Kir looked at each other and grinned. "Because we want you."

"Because we *need* you."

Kir moved to her left side and stretched out next to her. "Because we have to have you."

Logan lay down on her right and grinned. "Because we love you."

She gasped. "That's not possible. We've only known each other, what? Two days?"

"More like a week."

She glared up at him. "Barring the time I was unconscious. Or drugged."

"Damn. One of the reasons we fell in love with you was your stunning rendition of *Volare*."

Logan snickered. "Kir!"

Kir winked at him, then turned back to Jordan. "Haven't you ever heard of love at first sight?"

"Yes, I have, but both of you at the same time? Aren't the odds of that just a smidge on the high side of impossible, despite my stunning singing voice?" She held her hand up, thumb and forefinger a millimeter apart.

Logan snorted. "You're funny, you're brave, and you're beautiful. You're smart. You believed us when no one else did."

"Look, flame-boy, it's kinda hard to ignore the Incredible Igniting Man, ya know?"

The South Philly twang was back in her voice. He was coming to love that accent. He felt that wicked grin cross his face as he nestled in closer to her. "Why, thank you, ma'am." He let his hand rest on her stomach and flexed his fingers experimentally. "What else would you like to see me ignite?"

She rolled her eyes and turned to Kir. "Seriously. How do you put up with him?"

"He's really, really good in bed." He had to give Kir credit for saying it with such a straight face. That was one he never would have been able to pull off.

She looked up at the ceiling. "Great. I'm stuck between Perv and Pervier."

Logan held up a hand. "I get to be Pervier."

Kir laughed. "No argument here."

***

Jordan rolled her eyes and gritted her teeth as the idiots on either side of her laughed at their own cleverness. *Men.* "Guys!"

"Yes?"

"Hmm?"

She sighed. "Look, I have no idea what you're thinking, but *stop thinking it.*"

"No."

"Uh-uh. Sorry." Kir's hand moved to cup her breast. He ignored her squawk of protest as his thumb stroked her nipple through her shirt. "There isn't man alive who'd have a woman like you in his bed and not be thinking it."

"Unless he was gay," Logan added, gently prying her fingers off her shirt.

"True." Kir moved his hand long enough for Logan to pull her shirt open again. Goofy grins crossed both their faces as her breasts were exposed.

Damn, Logan's skin is so warm. She licked her lips, trying to focus her thoughts again on why this was a bad idea. She would have batted at him but Logan still had hold of her hand. "You're gods. Go do something, I dunno. Godly. And hands off, buster!"

"Sorry, I'm more of a hands-on kinda guy."

Jordan stared at Kir as Logan snickered next to her. She was starting to sense that Kir wasn't nearly as innocent as he tried to let on. "Why am I getting the feeling you're more the instigator?"

Kir gasped, doing his best to look innocent and failing miserably. The fact that his hand was still stroking her breast didn't help. "Me?"

"Yes, you! And you! Knock it off!"

Jordan turned to glare at Logan as he reached down and licked one bared nipple. She had the feeling that it lacked some impact when she gasped with pleasure.

"I'm sorry, but it was staring right at me. I had to do *something* about it."

She stared at him. "That was bad."

"I know."

"Humble doesn't work on you any more than innocent does."

"Give a guy points for trying?"

She twitched when a wet tongue licked her left nipple. "Kir!"

"Hmm?"

"Did you hear me say knock it off?"

"You said it to him, not me."

"Argh!"

"I think she's getting irritated."

Logan stared down at her thoughtfully. "No, see there? Her lips twitched."

"You're right. I think she likes us."

"I think so, too."

"I think you two are certifiable." She was trying desperately not to laugh.

"You think we're cute. Admit it." Kir was batting his lashes at her again. She had to bite her lip to keep the laugh in her throat.

"No!"

Logan tsk'd. "She said no again."

"Yeah, she did."

"What do you think she's saying no to?" Logan was inching his way down her body. She had the feeling that, unless she got a handle on things, her pants were going the way of the dodo.

"Guys! Hello! Been shot here! See? Owie!" She pointed to her arm in the sling. She blinked, realizing that her hand was free and she hadn't really tried to stop either of them from what they were doing.

"And we're offering to kiss your boo-boos but you keep saying that 'N' word."

"The one that ends in 'O'?" Kir's hand was still gently kneading her breast.

"Yup, that's the one." Logan's clever fingers were undoing her jeans.

Kir leaned over her with a leer. "Give up. Resistance is futile."

Logan's fingers stopped moving. He raised his eyebrow at Kir through the fall of his hair. "Didn't we agree there would be no more Borg in bed?"

"Oh, right. Sorry. Carry on."

These two are nuts! Incredibly sexy and hunk-a-licious, but nuts. "Oh, God."

"Yes?" They chorused.

"Get me out of here."

"Get you out of these? Sure!"

Logan's hands were incredibly gentle as he removed her pants and panties.

"I notice you're not really fighting." She looked up into Kir's suddenly serious face. "But if you really want us to stop, just say so."

Logan lay down next to her again and propped his head on his hand. "We *do* love you, you know." His other hand caressed her bared stomach again. His touch was soft and soothing. "We want you comfortable with us." His smile turned into a leer. "Of course, we'd like you hot for us, too."

The identical looks of hope on their faces melted her heart. "Guys…"

"Yes?"

"Hmm?"

Panic fluttered briefly in her heart. *I'm not ready for this yet. It's too damn soon.* "Give me time?" *Time to figure out what's really going on, and whether or not I want to be a part of it.* "Please. I'm not saying no, I'm saying wait. This…this isn't something I take lightly."

Logan looked at Kir over her naked body and smiled. "I can live with that."

"So can I." Kir leaned down and placed a soft kiss on her forehead.

They lay down next to her, Logan being extra careful of her wounded right shoulder. His erection pressed against her right hip, while Kir's pressed against her left. A wicked, sleepy grin crossed his lips. "G'night, John-boy."

Two groans were quickly followed by a dark chuckle. *Oh, man. What the hell am I doing?*

She'd just turned down sex with two of the most gorgeous men she'd ever met, but was still sleeping naked with them.

Jamie was going to have her committed.

Chapter Six

Kir leaned back against the base of the chaise lounge, his head resting against Logan's knee, and sighed contentedly. Jordan's head was resting in his lap, her gaze riveted to the plasma TV and the movie playing on it. *Bless you, Netflix.* Picking up *Bed of Roses* had been a stroke of genius. The female lead was just getting the idea that, perhaps, kicking Christian Slater out of her life had been the worst mistake she'd ever made. He was hoping Jordan's quick mind would pick up on the hint he was trying to give her.

Jordan frowned, and clicked the pause button. "I don't get it."

Logan leaned down and offered her another bite of s'more. "What don't you get, sweetheart?"

She swallowed before answering. Kir had the strongest urge to lean down and lick that little bit of chocolate that had escaped and was now decorating the corner of her mouth. "He does everything, and I mean *everything*, right, but she runs him off because she's afraid of being hurt." She shook her head, confusion all over her features. "I mean, how often do you find the perfect guy? And then to just send him away?"

Kir grunted. He'd already found the perfect guy, but he could kind of understand where what's-her-face was coming from. He picked up the box and read the actress's name: Mary Stuart Masterson. "Fear does weird things to some people."

"She fixes this, right? I mean, does he take her back?"

Kir took a bite of the s'more Logan held down for him and let his lover answer. "Wouldn't that be spoiling the movie?"

"But I want to know." She pouted up at them.

"Then watch." Kir shook his head sadly. "Are you one of *those* people?"

"*Those* people?"

"The ones who read the back of the book before they ever begin it."

She frowned. "There's nothing wrong with a little foreknowledge."

"If you say so." He grinned as Logan dropped the last bite of s'more into her mouth when she opened it to protest. "Do you want to watch the rest of the movie?"

Her eyelids were already drooping; the pain meds the doctors had her on were seriously sapping her energy. "I want to know what happens."

"Stay awake for a few more minutes, and you'll know." Kir started the movie back up, but didn't really watch it. He was too busy watching her, absorbing every nuance of her face and expressions as she sleepily watched the two lovers reconcile.

He heard a sniff above him and smiled. Looked like both the people he loved were suckers for a good chick flick. The moment Slater whispered, "Stay," both of them sniffled.

He thought about teasing Logan about what a girl he could be, but he didn't want *both* of them pounding on him.

The credits started rolling, and Jordan's eyes fluttered shut on a soft sigh. He sat patiently, not moving, waiting for her to fall asleep.

"I'll take her to bed." Logan stood, smiling down at the two of them. His eyes were suspiciously bright.

Kir waited until Logan picked Jordan up, careful of her wounded shoulder, and carried her to their room.

Their room. *Their* bed. It felt better every time he thought it. He stood up and quickly cleaned up the food wrappers and put the movie away, knowing Logan would come out to fetch him if he took too long.

Logan came back into the room quicker than Kir thought he would. He grabbed Kir by the back of the head and kissed him, long and hard. By the time he was done, two other things were long and hard, too. "Love you, babe. Gonna go take a shower."

Kir's chuckle was pained. He had a pretty good idea what Logan would do in the shower; the same thing Kir was planning on doing once he was done. "Bastard."

Logan tossed him a grin over his shoulder. "I'll save you some body wash, blondie."

He got a startled laugh when he flipped Logan the bird. He flopped back on the couch, grinning at how quickly the water turned on. He looked down at his tented sweatpants and laughed softly. "Wait your turn."

***

Two days later Logan rounded the corner to the kitchen to find Kir and Jordan in the kitchen. "Put it down."

The two started, looking towards him, guilt written all over their faces. "What?"

"If I have one more slice of pizza I'm going to start singing Sinatra songs."

Kir winced. Jordan stared at him curiously. "His singing voice sucks."

Logan rolled his eyes. "Out of my kitchen, people. I'll cook."

Jordan moved as quickly as she could out of his way. "Yum."

Kir sighed and followed her. "We could have spent this time cuddling, you know."

Logan tipped Kir's chin up and gave him a quick kiss. "Stop pouting, babe." He grinned down at his lover. "Jordan does it better."

"I heard that!"

Logan snorted. The girl had a set of lungs on her that would do a drill sergeant proud, a trait she and her sister seemed to share. However, the pain still in her voice was driving him mad. "Sit your pretty ass down and let me take care of the food, okay?"

"Asshole," he heard her mutter.

"Later, dear."

Logan looked at Kir in shock, not surprised to see the same expression on Kir's face. The twin echo of their reply still hung in the air as Jordan made her way back into the kitchen, practically snarling at the two of them.

She shook her finger at them, wincing a little with the movement. "I heard that! You two are a goddamn menace." She shook her head and left the kitchen, still muttering to herself as he and Kir started to laugh.

"Go make sure our girl stays put, would you?" Logan patted Kir's ass as he made his way out of the kitchen. He could hear them talking softly, Kir's voice low and soothing as he probably apologized for the comments in the kitchen.

"Oh, *God*."

The low, throaty moan caught his undivided attention. "Just a little to the right. Oh, yeah. *Right* there."

He stepped out of the doorway to the kitchen and peeked into the living room. He could see the top of Kir's head and his broad shoulders as he moved sinuously over what had to be Jordan lying on the sofa. Kir had his shirt off, all those muscles gleaming in the light coming in from the bank of windows.

Logan swallowed hard as another long, throaty moan sounded from the unseen Jordan. The look of sheer pleasure on Kir's face wasn't helping, either. "Just fucking kill me now, people."

Kir looked up, a wicked grin on his face. "Jordan's sore."

"Kir's got the most *incredible* hands I've ever felt."

He moved around the sofa to see Jordan sprawled boneless, face down on the sofa, her head pillowed in her arms. An expression of agonized bliss graced her face. She, too, was shirtless, clothes having become something of an optional accessory in the last week.

He knelt by her head and waited for her eyes to open. When she smiled at him, all sleepy and sensuous, he damn near came in his jeans. He leaned forward, sipping at her lips in gentle bites until she moaned and let him into the warm, wet cavern of her mouth. "Feel better, baby?"

"Mm-hmm." She sank even further into the sofa with a contented sigh. He couldn't help himself. He kissed her again, long, slow and languorous. He loved the feel of her moving under Kir's hands while he made love to her mouth.

She broke the kiss with a soft sigh. "Do you know something I've always wanted to do but didn't have the guts to try?"

I can think of about a dozen things I'd love to teach you that you've never tried, little girl. Logan shook his head. "No. What?"

"Mmm." She practically purred as Kir stroked her back. "Cooking."

Out of the corner of his eye he saw Kir's hands stop. He wasn't surprised at all when all three of them whimpered. "Cooking?"

"My mom is a really good cook, but I could never pick up the knack." She shifted under Kir, wiggling her ass against his jean-clad erection. Kir's swift intake of breath was swiftly followed by his shudder. "You're a fucking *fabulous* cook." The way she moaned *fabulous* had Logan practically panting.

The little tease.

She opened those sleepy eyes again and he was lost. "So, will you teach me?"

Logan knew she was manipulating him, but right at that moment he didn't care. If she wanted to play, that was fine by him. The time for playing was almost over. She accepted their hands on her skin, their kisses and touches, with ease. All she had left to do was accept their hearts, and if teasing and provoking them helped her do that, then bring it on.

Kir climbed off Jordan's back. "I'm going to go take a shower." He left, limping, more than likely hobbled by the erection Jordan had caused.

She wrinkled her nose. "I know cleanliness is next to godliness, but don't you guys take it a little *too* far?"

There really was no way to answer that, so he stood up. "Kitchen, you little tease."

"Oh, baby. Pass me the spatula." She stood, needing only a little help, threw her shirt back on and practically dragged him to the kitchen.

***

What the hell am I doing?

Jordan watched as Logan chopped onions, noting the ease with which he did so. His hands moved with confidence, his big body relaxed as he chatted with her. Even his erection didn't seem to bother him any, much to her surprise.

How do I tell him it's bothering the hell out of me*?* The urge to throw both men down on the floor and have her wicked way with them was getting stronger as she got better. She so desperately wanted a taste of them she was about ready to die if she didn't get it soon.

She couldn't quite figure out what had come over her back in the living room. Accepting Kir's offer of a massage had been totally innocent, but once he'd gotten his hands on her, she couldn't resist teasing them both. Hearing Logan moving into the room had just added fuel to the fire. It had become one of her favorite hobbies of late, watching the two men squirm.

She felt so comfortable around them both, like she could just let go and fly and they'd be there to catch her when she came back down. There wasn't anyone else she felt that way about, and it still had the power to frighten her.

She knew they were using her recovery time to win her over, and she also knew she was allowing it. If she wanted to leave, she knew she could, godly powers be damned. While they would try to persuade her otherwise they wouldn't try to stop her. No, she was staying as much for herself as for them. She *wanted* to see where this would lead, even if that meant she'd wind up with two men in her heart and her life.

And who the hell am I kidding? They're already there. She might lie to others, but she'd learned a long time ago not to lie to herself.

"And then I said, suck my cock, and he did."

Huh?

Jordan took her gaze off of his hands (and his dick) to see Logan smirking at her.

"Have you heard a single word I've said?"

Well, I heard 'suck my cock', but somehow I don't think it's wise to mention that. "Maybe?" She grinned and batted her lashes at him.

Logan snorted. "Right." He patted her on her rear. "Get me the green, yellow and red peppers out of the fridge, will you, sweetheart?"

She got the peppers, glad when she heard the water stop. "Are you going to take a shower now?"

Logan grunted. "Fucking tease."

She giggled as she dropped the peppers next to the onion.

The tangy smell of chili was beginning to fill the air as Kir came into the kitchen. He gave each of them an absent peck on the lips before lifting the lid off the pot. "Chili? Cool." He turned to Logan and bit his lip. "Shower's all yours."

Jordan couldn't help it. "You keep rubbin' at it it's gonna fall off."

She heard Logan choke on the beer he'd just opened.

She squeaked as Kir pushed her up against the countertop and took her lips in a wild, erotic kiss that curled her toes. "Don't worry, sweetheart. I'm a fertility god." He leaned forward just enough so that the next words were whispered against her lips, arching his hips so that his erection brushed against her in light, teasing strokes. "It's *not* going to fall off." He pulled away from her, winked, and sauntered out of the kitchen.

"Damn." She locked her knees to stop from hitting the floor.

"Amen." Logan leaned against the counter next to her, peering around to watch Kir as he sat at the dinette table. "My turn to get squeaky clean." He leaned in for his own kiss, and Jordan couldn't resist accepting him any more than she could have resisted Kir.

She pulled away from the kiss with a low laugh. "You are both *so* bad."

"Mm, but you love us anyway." It was his turn to saunter off, arrogance written all over his stride.

Damn. She hated it when arrogant men were right.

***

Grimm leaned back in his chair, a satisfied smile wreathing his face. It had taken him a while to unravel Loki's spell, but he'd finally succeeded. Now all he had to do was place his own spell on the video, and he'd have Loki right in the palm of his hand.

And when he had Loki, he'd have Baldur right where he wanted him.

Victory was going to taste oh, so sweet.

The knock on his door distracted him. He shut down the program and called, "Enter."

Val stepped into the room. "Sir, there are some security issues we need to deal with."

"Baldur and Loki?"

Val, the idiot, thought he could hide his emotions from his father, but the swiftly hidden grimace told its own tale. "No, sir. Simply business."

He settled back and listened while Val droned on, approving what the boy wanted with an impatient wave of his hand. No matter how incompetent the boy was in other areas, when it came to personal security Val was the best he'd run across. "Very well, implement the changes." He leaned forward, an eager smile on his face. "And prepare the special basement rooms for an extended visit, would you?"

The boy nodded, too swiftly for Grimm to get an accurate gauge of his feelings. "Yes, sir." He bowed his way out, not bothering to await further instructions. After all, the boy knew exactly what he wanted.

Grimm reopened the video and began weaving his own compulsion spell around it. He couldn't wait until Loki saw it. Once he did, Grimm would have him, and Baldur, in the palm of his hand.

***

Val stepped into the basement with a shiver. Here was where his father took care of problems that couldn't be handled with his "secret weapon". He only wished he knew what his father's secret weapon was; without that knowledge, he was helpless to stop whatever Grimm did to get the Aesir and Vanir to follow him so blindly. But the old man had made sure Val had no way to discover his secret.

Val reached out and stroked the side of the wooden cross, hoping against hope that whatever it was Grimm had planned, failed. He had to figure out what Grimm was up to, and he had to do it *fast*. Because if Grimm got someone into these rooms, they were never coming out again, except in a body bag.

A very small one.

***

"It's been two weeks. I think I can go home now."

Kir didn't even look up from his laptop. "Uh-uh."

"No."

She sighed and began pacing again. "I need to go to work."

"Uh-uh."

"No."

She growled. "I'm bored out of my tits and I'm going to start hurting people, especially people named *Kir* and *Logan*, if I don't get to *do* something!"

Kir kept his head down; no way did he want to get in the middle of the fight he sensed was brewing between his two lovers.

If they didn't stop bickering soon, though, he might be forced to kill them himself. Preferably with something dull and full of splinters.

"Play solitaire."

Her lip curled. "No."

"Go online and check your email."

"Kir has the laptop. That, and I already checked it today. *Five times*."

"Watch TV."

"Do you want to watch soap operas or home improvement shows? Because I don't."

"Fine. Jump out the window and see if you can fly."

Silence. Kir looked up to see Logan and Jordan glaring at one another.

"Are you two done?"

"No."

Kir pinched the bridge of his nose. They were giving him a headache. There had been no activity from Grimm and it was driving the two of them crazy. Add in the fact that Jordan was feeling better, and pushier, by the day, and one of them was going to snap.

When they weren't fighting, however, they were a blast to be around. Logan had decided to teach Jordan how to cook, with somewhat mixed results. Jordan's idea of a home cooked meal was a TV dinner with mashed potatoes in it. Truthfully, Kir wasn't much better. As far as he was concerned, pizza was the perfect food. And if you got the right toppings it hit everything on the food pyramid at the same time.

How could you go wrong with that?

They'd cuddled together, kissed each other…yeah, for the most part, things were going really well. They'd teased her with little flares of power, hoping to ease her into accepting that they weren't really human. Kir started it by bringing in a pot of mums and making them bloom just to make her smile after a really tough, painful day. Logan toasted marshmallows on little wooden skewers, using his inner flame and his fingers to brown everything to perfection.

They'd managed to turn bedtime into the best time of the day, despite the fact that they weren't having sex yet. Watching Logan and Jordan horse around in their huge bathroom, jostling each other for a spot at the same sink, was a hoot. Hips got bumped, asses got whacked with towels, and a tickle fight usually ensued. Logan was careful of Jordan's shoulder, too, stopping everything the minute she winced.

The three of them slept in the same bed, of course. Jordan had protested at first, but after two nights of being manually put to bed she'd given up fighting them on it.

Unfortunately, time was dragging on, and tempers were becoming shorter and shorter. She was very sore at first, wincing with every small movement of her shoulder, causing the two of them to treat her like spun glass. He could tell it was beginning to grate on her nerves, but neither one of them could live with her hurting herself again. She kept pushing and pushing, trying to do things that the doctor had told her were off limits for the time being. They'd even brought in a physical therapist so she wouldn't have to go to a clinic. She'd told Logan in private that, while she *was* making progress, Jordan was her own worst enemy. If she wasn't careful, she would overwork her shoulder, causing even more damage. Kir was just about ready to sit on her to get her to stop, and Logan was beginning to growl at any slightest movement. Her repeated request to leave so she could "get some work done", despite doctor's orders, was driving them ape-shit. Hell, even Jamie was getting fed up with her sister.

Today, the cooking lesson had been reduced to "Please pass the salt".

Add in the fact that he and Logan were horny as hell, and you had a volatile mix guaranteed to blow up. Having Jordan snuggle up to him in her sleep, then turn around and snuggle Logan, was driving them insane. He sighed wearily. *Man. This wooing crap sucks.* He made a mental note to pick up more body wash. They were going through it at an alarming rate. He had the feeling Logan was just as squeaky clean as he was. He'd ordered something online that would hopefully relieve their boredom, but it hadn't arrived yet. He wondered how long it would take them to convince Jordan to play the game naked.

The phone rang.

Then again... He grinned and stood, moving to the front door. "I think the present I got both of you may be here."

They stopped bickering and turned to stare at him. "What present?"

"You got us a present?" Logan bumped Jordan with his elbow. "Kir gets the *best* presents."

Kir was still grinning as he picked up the phone. "Hello?"

"Is this Kiran Tait?"

Kir sucked in a breath as the familiar voice washed over him. "Who is this?" *We're not ready yet, damn it! How did he find us?*

"I think you know."

"Hell."

"Please, don't hang up."

"Kir?" He felt Logan's hand on the small of his back. "What's wrong, babe?"

He put one hand over the receiver and stared at Logan, eyes wide. "Travis."

"I'd like to come up and speak to the three of you, if you don't mind." Travis Yardley-Rudiger's voice was soft and pleading. "Please."

"I don't think so!"

"I owe you both an apology, and I want to offer my assistance. Please, Kiran."

Logan must have heard Travis's words, because he frowned. "No *fucking* way."

"I don't blame Logan for being angry with me, but I think I can help."

Logan was shaking his head no when Jordan's hand passed them by and took the receiver. "C'mon up, Travis. We'll be waiting." She hung up the phone and stared at them both. "Don't worry; everything's going to be fine."

She started to walk away, Logan and Kir both glaring after her. "Why did you let him up?"

She turned, hands on hips, and tilted her head. "Am I right in thinking you two plan on me living with you indefinitely?"

"Try forever." Kir ground his teeth. *I have a bad feeling about this.*

"Does that make this my home?"

"Damn straight." Logan was frowning too.

She smiled sweetly. "Then that means I can have friends over. Right?"

"Jordan…" Kir didn't get a chance to finish the sentence, because the doorbell rang. Kir opened the front door to find a large blond man in a pair of dark blue jeans and a green polo shirt standing in the doorway. The big man stirred, his dark blue eyes searching behind Kir. "Jordan?"

"Hey, Travis!"

The man shoved his way inside the condo. Kir groaned as he saw the missing right hand. *Great. Just great.* He pinched the bridge of his nose again. The headache was getting worse.

"How the fuck did you get through the wards?"

Kir turned to see Logan standing in front of Jordan protectively, his eyes glowing infernally red. Jordan was waving and smiling at Travis.

Travis ignored Logan and focused on Jordan. "Are you in danger?"

She frowned. "No."

"You're here of your own free will?"

Uh-oh.

"Mostly."

"Mostly?"

Logan flicked a glance behind him. "Mostly?"

She rolled her eyes and stepped past him. "Logan, Kir, this is my boss, Travis."

"We know."

"We hired you, remember?"

She raspberried them, much to Travis's obvious relief. He relaxed visibly. "You're okay?"

"Not quite." As Travis tensed up again, Jordan walked over and pulled him into a hug.

It was Logan and Kir's turn to tense. "Jordan." He did *not* like seeing her hug other men. It made him want to growl and pound his chest like an idiot.

Or better yet, pound Travis until the other man let her go.

Travis glared at them over Jordan's head before turning his concerned gaze back down to her. "What happened? I get a hysterical email from Jamie claiming you were shot. You haven't been to your apartment in almost three weeks, there's a YouTube video that's driving Grimm nuts and a note to come visit you before you lose your mind and castrate someone. And what's this about you being 'not quite' okay?"

"Note?" Logan glared again at Jordan. "What note?"

She shrugged. "I wrote Travis and asked him to come here and take over the case."

"What?"

Logan's hissed disbelief echoed Kir's own emotions. *What is she talking about?*

"You guys obviously don't trust me to get the job done, so I called backup."

"It's not about trust, damn it!"

Kir ran his hands through his hair in frustration. "Logan's right. It has nothing to do with trust and everything to do with the bullet wound."

Travis, his arm protectively cradling the much smaller Jordan to his side, stared down at her. "Bullet wound? You *were* shot?"

"Guys, I'm okay! How many times do I have to wave my arms around to prove it?" She pushed away from Travis, jumping up and down and waving her arms around like a maniac. Kir saw the wince she tried to hide and had the urge to turn her over his knee.

"Stop hurting yourself!"

Kir winced at Logan's bellow. Flames were flickering around his body, leaving small scorch marks in the wood. He eyed the blackened marks and rolled his eyes. *Maybe we should have gone with stone or ceramic instead of maple.*

"Stop yelling at me!"

"Stop being a moron!" Logan threw his hands up in the air and growled. "I cannot fucking believe you think you can run out of the house and chase down fucking Grimm in his own fucking back yard and take him down three weeks after you've been fucking shot! Shit!"

Travis wiped his lips in a futile attempt to hide his grin. "Stubborn little thing, isn't she?"

Jordan gasped in outrage as Logan pulled his hair. "*Yes.*"

"I am not!"

Logan rolled his eyes. He bent his body, limping awkwardly in a circle. "No no, it's all right, it's only a flesh wound. I can run the marathon, clean the Empire State Building and still cure cancer before lunch! No problemo! Let me get right on that."

"I'm fine, Logan!"

Logan tapped his foot. "Who here thinks Jordan is just fine, raise your *right* hand waaaay over your head."

He raised both brows when Jordan tried, wincing as she did so.

"Oh, bite me, ass-wipe!"

Kir turned to Travis, ignoring the two bickering idiots in the middle of the hallway. "Coffee?"

"Love some, thanks."

"Follow me." He led the way into the kitchen and started making the coffee. "Has she always been like that?"

"Yes."

Kir turned to see Travis studying him closely. "How've you been, Tyr?"

"Frantic, not knowing where Jordan was. And call me Travis, please; Jordan doesn't know."

"I see she rectified that situation. And she doesn't know *yet*. Odds are she will soon."

Travis nodded, not looking entirely happy about that. "I know."

"Logan and I will have to have words with her about contacting you without consulting us first." He was no less pissed at Jordan than Logan was. He was just better at hiding it.

Travis's jaw clenched, but he didn't answer the taunt.

"Frankly I'm surprised you didn't come in guns blazing. Why didn't you?"

"A couple of reasons. First, Jordan asked me not to. She said the two of you were clients. She wants me to take over your case."

Before he could argue the term *clients*, he heard Logan move towards the kitchen. "Bullshit, Lefty." Logan pushed his way into the room and stood just in front of Kir. "She's not quitting, and I sure as hell don't want *your* help."

"Then why did you come to my agency?"

"Because we wanted Jordan. She just happened to work for you."

Logan was leering at Jordan, who rolled her eyes and stepped out from behind Travis. "Knock it off. Jerk."

"Get over here, Jordan."

Her eyebrows rose slowly at the commanding tone in Logan's voice.

"Now."

He could practically feel Logan vibrating between the need to protect both Jordan and himself, and having them so far apart made that impossible. "Please, Jordan." Kir held out his hand.

She sighed and stepped forward, taking his hand. He turned to Logan with a grin. "See? I told you she likes me better."

Logan gritted his teeth and smiled. "Right now I don't like either of you."

Kir turned to Travis. "What's your other reason for being here?"

Travis took a deep breath. "I owe you both an apology. A *big* one." He frowned, his gaze on Kir. "Can we discuss this in private?"

"I don't think so." Logan was still between Kir, Jordan and Travis.

Travis nodded, looking uncertain. "I meant with you and Kir."

"Why would you owe them an apology? You don't know them." Jordan's eyes blanked, a sure sign she was working something out in her mind. Travis grimaced just as she gasped. "Son of a *bitch!*"

Travis held up his hand, his expression pleading. "Now, Jordan, don't get mad, okay?"

"Travis Yardley-Rudiger? How could I not *see* that? That's almost as bad as *Grey!*" She glared at Travis. "Don't any of you have an original thought in your heads?"

"I do," Kir grinned, holding up a hand.

"Ditto."

Jordan turned her glare on Logan. "Oh, really, *Logan*?"

Kir smirked.

"Has anyone ever told me the truth? Anyone at all?"

The lost sound of her voice had him turning to her and pulling her into his arms. "Uh-huh."

"Yes. Of course." Logan's hands went around her waist as he cradled her to him, front to back. "We did the day we met you, remember?" His tone had gone from angry and resentful to soft and soothing. His gaze, still glued to Travis, was anything but soft.

Travis put his hand down. "Would you have believed me if I told you?"

Jordan stared at him for a moment. "Probably not." She pushed away from Logan and Kir and faced Travis. "But there are things you could have done to make me believe. Just like Frick and Frack here did."

"Hey!" Logan smacked her on the ass.

"Ow!" She rubbed the sore spot, glaring at Logan over her shoulder.

Kir sighed and pinched the bridge of his nose. If the two of them didn't knock it off, he was breaking out the splintery stick.

***

"I'm surprised you didn't offer to order in pizza, or to shine his boots." Logan sipped the extra-sweet coffee he favored and sneered at Kir over the rim of the mug. Kir was staring at Travis like he'd never seen the man before, and Jordan was sulking on the chaise, all curled up in herself and pouting at everyone equally.

"Shush." Kir waved a hand at him, ignoring Logan's snort. "You want to tell us what's *really* going on?"

"I saw the video." Travis shook his head, staring down at his coffee cup. "It was like a veil was lifted from my eyes."

Logan exchanged a quick look with Kir. "When was the last time you ate with Grimm?"

Travis looked up, confused. "What does that have to do with anything?"

"It has everything to do with everything." Logan sneered. "Or did you think your brain just suddenly started functioning again?"

Travis's eyes narrowed. "Oh, please. Are you telling me Grimm somehow has all of the Aesir and Vanir drugged or something?"

Logan nodded. "Yup, that about covers it."

Travis looked stunned, not that Logan gave a crap. "You've got to be kidding me."

"Just don't eat anything that might possibly have apple in it." Kir took a sip of his coffee, looking completely unconcerned.

Travis looked back and forth between the two of them. "*Apple?*"

"The golden apples of Idun? The ones that supposedly keep the gods eternally youthful? When the hell do you think dear old Grimm last allowed *us* a taste, hmm?"

Travis sat back, his brows lowered, his gaze turned inward. "He uses the apples to control the Aesir."

"Finally," Logan muttered, "someone gets it."

"Why didn't it work when Grimm wanted Guardian Investigations bought out by Grimm and Sons? I remember you ranting that it would be a cold day in Hell, blah blah blah." Logan looked over to see Jordan frowning.

Travis grimaced. "I'd been out of the country for a while, remember?"

"And you didn't attend any of the family dinners, and haven't been back since." Her legs uncurled and she sat up a bit, a good sign as far as Logan was concerned.

He was still going to spank her ass for calling Travis, however. From the look on Kir's face, he would have some help holding her down for it.

"I even remember how mad he was that you refused to share a drink with him."

The two of them stared at each other in grim understanding. Travis was the first to sit back. "Fuck. He's got all of them snowed."

"And docile. Remember, shepherds love sheep."

Travis stood and went to the laptop, Logan right on his heels. He wasn't having Travis messing around with their computer files and maybe finding out some things he wasn't ready for anyone, namely Jordan, to know yet.

Travis opened an internet connection and hopped over to YouTube, bringing up the video Logan and Kir had made. He frowned and clicked on something. "Seems like Grimm is trying to take your video down."

Logan snorted. "Yeah, good luck with that, Old Man."

Travis stood. "I gather you have some sort of spell on the video?"

Logan shrugged. "Of course." He took a sip of his coffee, staring over the rim at Travis. He wanted the other man to understand that, as far as Logan was concerned, he was still here under protest.

"Be nice, Logan."

He turned and stared at Jordan, who was frowning at him again. He was getting damn tired of her frowning at him. "Why the hell should I?"

"This is Grimm's fault not," she waved her hand at Travis and grimaced, "Tyr's."

"Travis." Travis was staring at something on the computer screen as he corrected her.

"Whatever." She shook herself all over. "This is getting more bizarre by the moment, you know that, right?"

Logan snorted.

"I mean it, Logan. Travis isn't just my boss, he's my friend."

He ground his teeth together.

She raised her eyebrow and cocked her hip, like she expected him to just give in and play nice with the enemy.

"He was under the influence of the apples, just like the rest of them." She tilted her head. "Doesn't that mean I'm the enemy, too?"

"No!"

"Uh-uh!"

"But I had the apples, too, remember? If Grimm had decided to tell me to, I dunno, marry Magnus or Morgan, I'd be a Grimm right now." Her face paled. "What if he'd called my cell phone and ordered me to kill you? Wouldn't I have to obey?"

All three men were shaking their heads before she'd finished. "You'd need a bit more persuasion than that." Logan walked over to her and took her hand. "He'd have to have you under the influence, and then explain things to you in such a way that you believed them utterly."

"So it's more like you're highly suggestible, not really completely under his control?"

"Exactly."

"Oh. So how did you break free?"

He grinned, knowing how cold he looked and not caring. "Why do you think we didn't get along all that well?"

"It didn't work on you?"

"Oh, it worked, all right." Logan sat on the chaise and pulled her into his lap, curling his hand around her hip. She settled down absently against him, making herself comfortable, a fact neither Kir nor he missed. They'd lived with her long enough to know that her temper burned bright but swift, especially if you could engage her curiosity. "But I figured it out and started *pretending* to eat. The effects wore off."

"Enabling you to save Kir when no one else could."

He nodded. Kir was smiling, Travis looked disturbed, and Jordan was grinning. "Damn, I knew you were clever."

He rolled his eyes. For a millennium or more he'd *defined* clever.

When her lips brushed his cheek he stilled. It was the first spontaneous, freely given display of affection she'd bestowed on either of them. He grinned at Kir and mouthed, *See? She likes me better.*

Kir chuckled.

"Travis, any idea what we can do next? Until Tweedledee and Tweedledum allow me out of the condo there isn't much I can do other than online stuff." She glared at Kir and Logan equally. "Which is why I called you in."

Travis opened his mouth to answer when a knock sounded on the front door. They stared at it.

"Kir?"

"I didn't order in pizza, Logan, honest."

Logan tensed as Kir went to answer the door, setting Jordan back on the sofa and standing quickly. "Kir!" He strode towards his lover.

"I know, I know! Sit, Kir. Stay. Woof." Kir leaned against the wall and crossed his arms.

"Don't pout, babe. Jordan does it better." Logan opened the front door with a grin.

The punch hurt almost as much as Jordan's piercing shriek. He looked up from his position on the floor to see the twin sons of Thor standing over him, fists clenched, murder in their eyes.

"How the *fuck* did you get through the wards?"

Kir pushed both men back, ignoring their futile attempts to land a blow on him. "Gentlemen, if you'll just calm down, I'm certain we can come to some sort of understanding."

"Die, imposter!" Magnus Grimm threw another punch, looking startled when it glanced off that invisible shield Kir was endowed with.

"Die!" Morgan Grimm echoed his brother's movements a split second after, with the same effects.

Logan leaned up on his elbows and glared at them. "Again, I ask: *How did you get through the fucking wards?*"

"You must be slipping, Loki. There are no wards." Magnus glared down at him, his blue eyes fierce, his face nearly matching his red hair as he tried to land blow after blow on Kir and failed.

Morgan managed to get behind Kir and began raining blows on the back of his head. If he'd succeeded in landing just one, Kir would have been unconscious. Instead, he looked like the world's largest bobblehead, as the repeat blows bounced his head forward.

"*Guys!*" Jordan bellowed, her hands cupped around her mouth. "Stop!"

"Did they hurt you?" Morgan bellowed back, turning to stare at her. He kicked Logan's leg in the process, looking grimly delighted when Logan hissed in pain.

Logan stood. He felt his fires building inside him. *Oh, goody. I haven't had a really good fight in a long, long time.* His smile was feral as his fists lit up. "Hey, pretty boy. Did Daddy send you out here to do his dirty work?"

"Logan, knock it off."

"Tell that to your stepbrothers, Jordan." He and Morgan began to dance around one another, both waiting for the other to make the first move.

"Really, Magnus, you'd think you'd know me. You're my damn nephew, after all." Kir was still trying to hold off Magnus, the elder twin, with little luck; neither one of them was willing to let the twins anywhere near Jordan, which was severely hampering their movements.

Morgan, the bastard, feinted left, and Logan fell for it. He got past Logan, pulling Jordan behind him, both of her wrists grasped in one big hand. "We're leaving now, sis."

Jordan gasped in pain as Morgan, all unknowing, put pressure on her shoulder wound.

Thunder cracked. Lightning struck just outside the building, blinding anyone who looked out the window. Kir turned, his eyes dark blue, the irises white as snow. Dark clouds drifted across their surface like reflections in a pond. He completely ignored Magnus' last punch; his head didn't even move. "Get your hands off of her. *Now*."

Logan shivered at the low timber of his lover's voice. *Shit. Baldur's been roused.* From the sheet of rain that was suddenly coming down outside, Kir was severely pissed.

Magnus' eyes were wide, but he refused to let go, holding Jordan behind him despite her desperate attempts to get free. "No. I refuse to hand my sister over to a murderer."

Kir's eyes closed and his head tilted back.

Logan felt a chill go down his spine as power built around Kir. "Kir, no."

When Kir opened his eyes, a spring storm, grey and white and blue all swirled together, danced across them. They were totally inhuman. Light pulsed around him, dappled green as the light that shone through new leaves. *"Let her go."* His voice was the softest and most dangerous Logan had heard in centuries.

Morgan and Magnus both looked confused at Kir's display. "That's not possible," Magnus whispered, moving around the glowing Kir. "It has to be a trick."

"No trick." Logan stood slowly and approached Kir, his eyes never wavering from his lover's face. The last time he'd seen that look on Kir's face was when he'd found Logan tied to the mountain. "Love?"

Kir blinked, some of the anger receding from his face, but his gaze remained riveted to Morgan.

"Morgan? You need to let go of Jordan now." Travis stepped carefully between Kir and Morgan, gently pulling Jordan's hands out of Morgan's grasp.

"It has to be a trick." Magnus pushed Logan aside and tried to touch Kir.

Before Logan could react, light flashed, thunder sounded, and Magnus was flying across the room. His unconscious body slammed into the wall, cracking the drywall. A blackened spot on the maple floors attested to where the lightning had struck, only inches away from Magnus.

Fuck. He'd *never* seen Kir do *that.*

"Don't ever touch Logan again." Those stormy eyes drifted back to Morgan. He looked coldly indifferent. "Care to take a turn?"

"Kir?" Logan got between them again, knowing how close his lover was to losing it. Kir wasn't a killer, and Logan wasn't about to allow him to become one now. "We're safe now, blondie."

Kir shook his head slowly. "No, we're not. The wards are down."

Logan blinked and looked over Kir's shoulder. "No they're not." He blinked again and frowned. "Yes, they are."

He turned slowly and glared at Jordan, who looked confused. "What?"

"You took the wards down."

"I did not!"

Logan snorted. "You did so."

"Did not!"

"Children." Kir's voice was lazily amused. "Play nice."

Logan started to turn and answer him when, out of the corner of his eye, he saw Morgan lift a gun.

The barrel was aimed right for Kir.

"No!" Logan dove, trying to get between Kir and the bullet.

Everything seemed to happen at once. Morgan went flying back, the bullet missing Kir by a good foot. Jordan screamed again as Travis let go of her. His hand was out, fingers spread, encasing both Morgan and Magnus in cages of force. The larger man was also glowing.

Travis turned glowing, blind eyes on Logan and Kir, his gaze unfocused. "Justice has been a long time coming for the two of you." He grinned, a self-mocking expression that Logan was all too familiar with. He'd seen it in his own mirror one too many times. "But I'm here now." He turned to the two young men groggily getting to their feet, identical expressions of hatred on their faces. "Don't worry about these two; I'll take them off somewhere where they can get over the effects of Grimm's drugs, then I'll do my best to pound some sense into them."

"Um, Travis?"

"Yes, Jordan?"

She gestured towards her eyes. "You might wanna, you know, wear your sunglasses when you leave." The men looked at her, and she shrugged. "What? I'm just sayin'." She took a deep breath and turned to Kir with a shaky grin. "Want to order in pizza?"

Logan exchanged a look with Kir, grateful to see his eyes had returned to normal. She'd seen almost all there was to see of them, and she wasn't afraid.

He was done waiting. As soon as Travis and the others left, her ass was theirs.

Chapter Seven

The door shut quietly behind Travis, with Morgan and Magnus in tow, magical leashes around their necks and wrists. Logan leaned back, studied the door intently, and made a few graceful gestures with his hands.

Something glowed on the edges of Jordan's vision, settling back down into nothingness when Logan was done.

It never failed to amaze her when they used their powers around her. They were so ordinary otherwise that, when they *did* act otherworldly it was a bit of a shock. Kir's "temper tantrum" of a storm was still raining all over the city, and there were fresh scorch marks in the wood where Logan had been standing.

Logan turned and exchanged a look with Kir, his head leaning against the door. The way Logan was shaking his head worried Jordan. His shoulders were tense, but she could just see the corner of his mouth, and it was turned up.

Kir wasn't much better. He was leaning up against the wall with his arms crossed. His expression was hungry as he stared at her. The heat in his gaze nearly burned her. She licked her lips, her heart beating faster as his gaze locked on her mouth.

Logan turned around, leaned against the door, and crossed his arms over his chest. If Kir's expression was hungry, Logan's was predatory.

Her gaze darted back and forth between the two men, reading trouble there. She knew how difficult the last few weeks had been on them. The men hadn't sought relief with one another, despite how hot they'd all made each other. She also knew they weren't truly angry with her. She'd been here long enough to see how both men reacted when they were pissed, and this wasn't it. From the looks of things, they were definitely more horny than irritated. *Looks like my time's up.* An erotic shiver went down her spine. She still couldn't believe she'd lasted as long as she had. Maybe part of her recent bitchiness was her own frustration peeking through. Truth be told she was just as tired of waiting. "Uh, guys?"

"You took the wards down." Logan started forward, his arms moving easily by his sides. His stride was lazy, his gaze hooded as he stalked towards her.

She shook her head. "I really have no idea what you're talking about." She started to inch back as Kir pushed off from the wall and began circling towards her. He glided around the chaise and the ottoman, his eyes never leaving her.

She felt the brush of Logan's fingers against her cheek and yelped. She whipped around to find him right on top of her. "I think I know which one of my gifts you received." He took her arm and began steering her backwards towards the chaise. "How badly did you want to see Travis?"

Pretty damn bad, but she wasn't about to tell *them* that. "He's my friend as well as my boss. And I called him here."

"You didn't just create a pass-through for Travis, Jordan; you took *all* the protections down."

She gulped. "I don't know magic, Logan. How would I do that?"

Logan grinned, the expression all teeth. "I'll explain later. First, Kir and I are going to make sure you're too damn busy to email anyone else." He leaned in close, nearly distracting her from Kir, who'd come up behind her.

Kir's hands settled on her waist, his lips teasing the side of her neck. His lips slowly moved up her neck to lick delicately at the shell of her ear. She could feel her brain shutting down as images of her in a heavenly sandwich began overriding everything else. From the look in their eyes, her days of putting them off were officially over, and while her mind said *wait a minute*, her body was singing the Hallelujah Chorus. "Uh, are the wards back up?"

Logan's hands began unbuttoning her blouse. "Yup." The feral heat in his eyes had her heart pounding. "Don't worry, sweetheart. We won't be interrupted."

He pushed her shirt off her shoulders, Kir taking over to pull it off her arms. "No?"

"No." He took her mouth in a kiss designed to set her soul on fire. She felt Kir gripping the back of her head, pulling her gently to the side. Logan moaned in response.

"My turn." Kir's mouth descended, ravaging hers in a kiss that rivaled Logan's. He broke off, licking his lips. "Sweet."

"Mm-hmm." Logan hummed his response against the curve of her breast as he nibbled down towards her nipple.

When did I lose my bra? Wait. When did I lose my shirt?

She felt Kir kneel behind her, taking her jeans and panties with him. When he nipped at one of her ass cheeks she gasped.

"Like that, sweetheart?" Logan took her nipple gently between his lips and sucked, the sensation rocketing down to her clit.

"Oh God," she moaned, arching into the gentle bite of Logan's teeth.

"Yes?" the two men chorused.

She stared up at Logan, who was looking down at her with something more than just heat. She turned her head slightly and felt Kir rub his cheek against hers like an affectionate cat, the whiskers of his five o'clock shadow abrading her skin.

For two weeks they'd teased, touched, laughed, and kissed, but hadn't gone beyond that. They'd shown her both the good and the bad of living with them.

Now she couldn't picture living without them.

She reached up and caressed Logan's cheek, leaning her own cheek against Kir's.

Logan turned his head and kissed her palm. "I think that's a yes."

The relief in his voice made her smile.

"I think so, too."

She laughed, and nodded. "Yes."

She never saw two men strip so fast in her life. Kir was the first to lose his clothes, tripping and falling down on the chaise as he tried to remove his shoes and pants at the same time. He scooted further up the chaise after exchanging a wicked look with Logan.

Jordan gasped when Logan put her on the chaise, straddling Kir's calves. He gently pushed the back of her head, putting her lips down to Kir's cock, lifting her hips at the same time. She blushed, knowing the view he was getting of her wet pussy. "Suck him, baby."

Kir was staring down the length of his body, his hand gently stroking her hair as he looked at her with a hot, pleading look. "Please."

That quick laughter turned to a need so raw her pussy wept from it. She grabbed the base of his cock and lifted it up, licking around the flared head in slow, lingering swipes. His slow hiss as he lifted his hips was music to her ears.

She moaned when Logan's fingers circled her clit. "Take him in, sweetheart. I want to watch you make him come."

"Oh, shit." Kir's eyes went wide as Jordan took him as far down as she could go. His eyes rolled back in his head as she sucked as hard as she could, his moans and gasps of pleasure spurring her on.

A wet tongue lapped at her pussy. "It's been a very long time since I've had a woman." Logan's voice was dark and rich with need. "And I intend to enjoy every—" *lick* "—last—" *lick* "—long—" *lick* "—minute of it."

She groaned as Logan settled in behind her, sucking on her clit as she tongued the underside of Kir's cock. Kir grabbed both sides of her head as she bobbed up and down on him. She made sure to keep her tongue hard against the underside of his cock, something he seemed to appreciate if his moans were anything to go by.

Nothing made her hotter than a man who let her know he was enjoying himself.

Logan stopped sucking on her and stood, leaning over her back. One hand continued to play her clit while the other hand landed on the chaise, holding him steady. She could feel the warm head of his cock lodge between her thighs, brushing her wet core. She pushed back a bit, trying to get him inside her.

The slap on her ass tingled and made her jump. "Naughty girl. Not yet." Logan's tongue lapped the crease of Kir's thigh and groin, making Kir cry out. The agonized pleasure on the blond man's face was a sight to behold.

She bucked back onto Logan's hand as he inserted what felt like two fingers into her pussy. She reached around and stroked his cock, resting against her hip, until he pulled away from her.

"No. Kir first, then I get mine." His mouth went back to Kir's balls, tonguing them while she sucked.

"Oh, shit, oh shit, oh *shit*!" Kir bucked up into her mouth and came down her throat, one hand clenched in her hair, the other clenched in Logan's.

"Mmm, nice," Logan purred, pulling his mouth off Kir's balls. He put one knee on the chaise and leaned over, kissing Kir long and hard.

He turned to Jordan. "Your turn."

Logan helped Kir up off the chaise while Jordan watched, wide-eyed. "My turn?"

Kir chuckled. "You didn't think we would leave you wanting, did you?" He picked her up and laid her gently on the chaise. "It's simple, really." He plucked her hard nipples with his fingers as Logan went down on her again, lapping at her like a starving man. "Logan's going to eat you until you come, then I'm going to fuck you while you suck his cock."

"Hey!" Jordan looked down to see Logan frowning at Kir. "Who says you get to fuck her first?"

"I do." He was grinning at Logan, who leaned against Jordan's thigh with a cocky look on his face.

"I think I should get to fuck her first."

The two glared at one another, then grinned. "One, two, three, shoot!"

"Damn." Kir threw his head back and laughed. "Looks like you get to fuck her first."

Jordan stared at the two men who'd just played Rock Paper Scissors for the right to take her first. "You're kidding me, right?"

Logan dived right back in, sucking on her clit until the argument, and how they'd handled it, was blown right out of her head. Kir was suckling her nipples, one right after the other, the sensation almost more than she could bear. Then Logan worked a little of his magic, heating his tongue just a little bit more than a normal human could do. It was if he'd sipped hot coffee then immediately gone down on her. The added sensation threw her over the edge.

She came, clenching Kir to her breasts as she bucked up against Logan's mouth with a shuddering moan.

Kir kissed her as Logan eased her down off the orgasm, lapping at her mouth as gently as Logan lapped at her pussy.

Logan sat back on his heels and wiped his mouth with the back of his hand. "Ready, sweetheart?"

She fell back with a laugh; she was still seeing stars from the orgasm he'd already given her. "Not really, no."

He looked at Kir, who had started stroking his growing erection, and bit his lip. "Want to watch?"

Kir's hand stopped. His gaze went from Logan to Jordan and back again.

Can I really watch the two of them together?

She'd read some male/male erotic romances before, gifts from Jeff, and had liked them a lot more than she thought she would. And this would be the real test; she knew if she couldn't completely accept this side of their relationship she would lose both Logan and Kir.

The thought of losing either one of them left her feeling cold and alone.

Logan crawled over to Kir and reached out a hand. Kir watched as both he and Logan stroked Kir's cock. Jordan felt her arousal begin to build all over again as the two of them pleasured Kir. She looked up into Kir's face and saw him watching her, anxiety warring with his pleasure. She had the urge to reach over and begin stroking him herself, just to reassure him.

Hell. This must be love.

***

Kir looked down at his lovers, keeping a careful eye on Jordan to make sure she was handling what she was seeing.

When Logan's warm, wet tongue lapped the head of his cock he had to close his eyes. The sensation was incredible, different from the feel of Jordan doing the same. Where she'd lapped slowly, savoring him, Logan devoured, intent on gobbling every last bite.

And with Logan he could be a little bit rougher. He grabbed the sides of Logan's head and forced his cock down Logan's throat, moaning at the sight of his length disappearing between Logan's greedy lips. He began fucking his lover's mouth steadily, watching his wet cock glide between those red lips.

"Oh, wow," Jordan breathed. Her small, delicate hands began gliding up and down Logan's back. "Okay, that's a lot hotter than I thought it would be."

She began marking Logan with little nipping kisses up and down his back as he sucked on Kir's cock. Logan moaned around him, making Kir gasp.

Fuck, he wasn't going to last very long at this rate.

"Oh, fuck." Logan's eyes were squeezed shut. Kir looked down and saw Jordan jacking him off, one hand running up and down his cock, the other cradling his balls.

"She's got an even better mouth, love." Kir smiled, watching Logan writhe under Jordan's hands.

Logan looked up with a hot grin. "Fuck that shit." Kir toppled back as Logan pushed him, hard. He landed on his back on the chaise again. "Up you go!" Logan took Jordan's hands and put her over Kir, sixty-nine style.

Oh, I like where this is going. Kir grinned as he took a hold of Jordan's hips, holding her steady as Logan entered her on one long, slow thrust.

Jordan took him back into her warm, wet mouth with a greedy moan. She sucked him down as Logan set up a steady rhythm, his balls slapping up against her with a wet sound.

Kir lapped at her clit and she quivered, making Logan gasp and lose his rhythm. With a wicked grin Kir made sure that at least some of his licks hit Logan on the balls as Jordan devoured his cock.

He couldn't help himself, it felt so damn good. He bucked up into Jordan's mouth, feeling the wet heat, watching Logan fuck her from below.

Oh, yeah, not gonna last long at all.

He reached down and grabbed a hold of Jordan's head, steadily fucking her mouth while he suckled her erect clit. Her long, drawn out groan as she came above him nearly had him spilling down her throat.

It was a good thing Logan had had Jordan give him that blow job. Logan could go all fucking day without coming if he wanted. Kir, on the other hand, needed something to take the edge off.

"Oh, yeah. Again. Do that again."

Kir began lapping once more at Jordan as Logan began fucking her harder. He tried to concentrate on what he was doing to them, afraid if he paid too much attention to his cock he would blow before he was ready.

He had every intention of blowing his next load in Jordan's hot, wet pussy.

He ran his hands up and down her back, his fingers tangling with Logan's.

This was even better than he'd dreamed. The two people who meant the most to him in the world, the three of them in one big, happy knot as they made love to one another.

The feel of Jordan's mouth was driving him insane. And watching Logan fuck her?

Damn.

She was moaning around his cock again, driving him insane. He couldn't help himself. He reached around again, holding her head steady while he fucked her mouth. He was so damn close…

He howled as he came down her throat again. He fell limp, panting for breath, eyes closing as Logan stroked slowly in and out of Jordan.

He collapsed with a laugh as Jordan licked him clean. *Well, hell.* Guess he'd have to wait to feel her pussy around him, but he really couldn't find it in himself to complain too much.

***

Jordan leaned back and did her best to swallow Kir's come. He didn't taste human. He tasted like springtime, and fresh water, and everything sweet, like nectar. She'd never been a huge one for giving blow jobs, but damn. Any time Kir wanted one, she was so there.

"You like that, sweetheart? You want more?"

She shuddered as Kir pulled her hips down, lapping again at her clit.

"Now you know one of the reasons I love fucking him. He's so damn delicious."

The naughty words sent a shudder through her. Logan picked up the pace as he felt it. "You gonna come for me again, sweetheart?"

She felt it begin again, that slow build up that heralded her orgasm, her whole body clenching and unclenching. Her head dropped to Kir's hip as he suddenly pulled her clit into his mouth and sucked, hard.

She came screaming, her toes curling, her nails digging into Kir's thighs as she rocked back against Logan.

"Oh, *shit.*" Logan moaned and grabbed her hips, thrusting in and out of her so rapidly she was surprised she didn't light on fire.

"Oh, fuck, yeah, come, Logan."

Kir's deep voice seemed to send Logan over the edge as he exploded in her still quivering pussy, his deep shout echoing off the walls. The hot, wet warmth of his come bathed her womb.

Logan's hands landed on either side of her and Kir, his breathing deep and harsh. Kir let her go with one last, soft lick, letting her complete her collapse onto his body.

"No fair, Kir. That was foul play."

She could feel Kir smiling against her inner thigh. "I want my turn, remember?"

Logan snorted. "Shoving your finger up my ass and making me come gets you your turn?" He twisted and collapsed onto the chaise, pulling her with him, so that he cradled her body against him.

Kir grinned happily and petted Jordan's leg. He looked ready to purr. "I know you. You'd have stayed there all day if I let you."

"Would I have had any say in this?" Jordan wheezed. She was still trying to catch her breath after three of the most intense orgasms of her life.

"No."

"Uh-uh."

Jordan snorted.

Kir laughed so hard he fell off the chaise.

Chapter Eight

Kir reached over, feeling for Logan and Jordan. Neither one of his lovers were in bed. He wondered if the morning fun had started without him. He grinned and opened his eyes, picturing the two of them together on the chaise in the living room, devouring each other's bodies.

"Blech!"

He tilted his head, surprised at the disgust in Jordan's voice. He got up and padded naked out of the bedroom to see what was going on.

"Just try it. You might like it."

Oh, curiouser and curiouser. They weren't in the living room. *Where, oh where have my lovers gone?* He was in an incredibly good mood, probably due to the incredibly good sex they'd had the night before.

He was looking forward to round two (or was that three?) today.

"And I might like having my legs shaved with a chainsaw, but somehow I doubt it."

That's coming from the kitchen. He peeked around the edge of the doorway to see Logan holding a tiny cup towards Jordan.

"C'mon. I think you'll like espresso."

Jordan put her hands on her hips. "Espresso is just a fancy name for liquid road tar. Can't you fix me something that tastes better? Like puree of two-day-dead skunk?"

"You have to know what espresso tastes like if you're going to cook with it."

"Then I won't cook with it."

"Don't you want to learn how to make things like tiramisu?"

She looked at Logan like he was very, very stupid. "Haven't you heard of the Italian Market? Hello! Bakeries!"

Logan shook his head and drank the espresso.

Kir leaned his head on the doorframe and started laughing. *Looks like the cooking lessons are back on.*

"What the hell are you laughing at, blondie?"

Kir walked out of the kitchen, shaking his head. "I'm going to take a shower. Anyone want to join me?"

"Ooh, hot blond wetness? Count me in!"

Logan ran past him to the bedroom, shedding clothes as he went.

"Nah, I'm going to make a pot of coffee and check my email while the laptop is free. Okay?"

Kir looked back and saw Jordan fiddling with the coffeemaker. "You sure?"

She looked up and smiled at him lazily. "Yeah. I need my caffeine fix. You two, um, enjoy yourselves." She waggled her eyebrows, her cheeks heating.

He walked back to her, enjoying the way her eyes roamed down his body to lock on his cock. When she licked her lips he had to stifle a groan. He tilted her face up and leaned forward, planting a soft kiss on her lips. "Are you *sure* you're okay with all of this?"

"If you keep asking me I'm going to start wondering if *you're* okay with all of this."

His smile was heated as he replied, "I have a redhead waiting in the shower and a brunette waiting for me in the kitchen. Trust me, I'm okay with it."

"Hmm, tough choice, huh?" She rubbed her cheek against his hand affectionately.

"Kir! Get your ass in here before I use up all the hot water!"

Kir rolled his eyes. Jordan laughed and pushed him out of the kitchen. "You'd better hurry up or the hot water won't be the only thing Logan uses up!"

Kir stopped, turned, and grabbed her hand. "I have an idea." He dragged her towards the bedroom.

"So do I, and it involves a coffee mug and Gmail."

"Trust me, this is better." He heard Logan splashing in the shower. *Perfect.* He pulled Jordan in behind him and closed the door. He picked her up and sat her down on the countertop, ignoring her pout. He leaned on the countertop, arms braced on either side of her body. "Choose."

"Um. Maxwell House?" She grinned up at him weakly.

He leaned in and whispered in her ear. "Choose. Do I suck Logan off, or do I fuck him?"

He saw her look over his shoulder and turned. Logan was staring at them and slowly stroking his erection.

She gulped and took a deep breath. Then she leaned in to whisper in his ear. He could feel her body trembling against him and he closed his eyes in gratitude. She was turned on. Her rich, feminine smell and her tiny, tell-tale shivers made him want to lick her all over. "If you fuck him and you both come, who will fuck me?"

Kir leaned back and matched her grin for grin.

***

Logan watched his two loves share identical heated grins, his hand stroking up and down his cock. *Yum. Looks like Kir wants to play and he's gotten Jordan to go along with it.*

He relaxed back against the shower wall, content for the moment to let his lovers play with him. He'd sneaked out of bed late last night and reinforced the wards, just in case Jordan somehow "accidentally" wiped them away again. Their home was as safe as he could make it.

Home.

His hand paused as Kir entered the shower with him. His free hand tangled in the damp strands of Kir's hair as Kir started nibbling at his neck.

He saw Jordan begin to remove her clothes, a wicked little smile on her face, and his heart lurched.

Yes. Home.

He moaned as Kir sank to his knees in front of him. He felt the wet swipe of Kir's tongue on the underside of his cock and shivered. He kept his eyes on Jordan, watching her reactions, letting her see his. Her skin was flushed, her breath coming faster as she watched Kir pleasure him with his tongue.

Kir sucked him down, taking him to the root, and the back of Logan's head hit the shower wall with a thump. He kept his eyes open through sheer force of will, wanting to watch Jordan, but it was a damn hard thing to do when Kir's tongue was lashing the head of his cock.

Kir took him back down his throat again, his eyes closed as he hummed in appreciation. Logan hissed at the added sensation, his hips thrusting forward in an involuntary movement. He pulled back, trying not to choke Kir, but Kir pulled on both his hips and swallowed him down as far as he would go.

"Holy fuck." Logan wasn't going to last long if Kir kept that up. He looked down to see Kir's heated gaze locked on his face as he pulled back slowly. His tongue felt incredible, his mouth wet and warm. He couldn't help himself; he grabbed the sides of Kir's head and slowly sank between those warm lips. "Are you gonna let me fuck you, babe?"

Kir shook his head.

"No?" Logan sank deeper, hitting the back of Kir's throat. "You want me to come in that pretty mouth?"

Kir nodded.

Logan turned his head and looked at Jordan through the fall of his wet hair as he slowly fucked Kir's mouth. She was playing with her nipples, staring at where the two men were joined, her eyes glazed with passion.

Logan grinned. "Jordan?"

She looked up and licked her lips.

"What do you want, sweetheart? Both of us, or one of us?"

"Huh?"

It was a good thing he had a hold of Kir's head, because Kir stopped moving. Logan didn't. "Should I come in Kir's mouth, or are you up for something different?" And she'd better decide soon, because Kir was engulfing his cock again, all the way... *Damn.*

Jordan bit her lip, her gaze once more caught by the sight of him fucking Kir's mouth. "I want..." She cleared her throat. "I want to watch."

Logan's grin turned feral as he moved his hands. One went to the back of Kir's head, gathering the wet strands, moving him in a sure rhythm his hips matched.

The other gestured Jordan closer, and she came, her body moving like a wet dream. He reached out with his free hand and cupped her breast, rolling the nipple between two fingers.

Kir's fingers stroked past his perineum to stroke his hole, and Logan knew he wasn't going to be allowed to last much longer. He leaned to the side and took Jordan's nipple into his mouth just as Kir's finger entered his anus, fucking into him in sync with his mouth. He bit and nipped gently, enjoying Jordan's gasps. Her hands flew to his head, holding him in place. He matched his sucking to Kir's, moaning around her flesh as Kir found his prostate. He could feel his balls pulling up, the tingling down his spine signaling his impending orgasm.

When Kir hummed again he lost it, coming in his lover's mouth with a loud groan. He released Jordan's nipple, falling against the shower wall as Kir sucked him dry.

He collapsed in the tub as his knees gave out. "Shit, babe." He laughed as Kir bent and gave him one last, long lick, the smug look on his face amusing as hell. He reached out and stroked Kir's cheek. "Love you, babe."

"Love you, too."

"I wanna watch you fuck Jordan now."

Kir looked up at Jordan, the look on his face hotter than any fire Logan had ever started. "My pleasure." And he stood with a grace and power that had Logan shivering in renewed desire.

***

Jordan gulped as Kir slinked out of the shower, hard, hot cock dripping wet from the water and waving menacingly in front of him.

When he held up one hand and crooked his finger, she nearly ran for it. Some primal instinct inside her told her that this was more than just a fucking from two hot men; this was a claiming, the two of them forever putting their stamp on her.

Like they didn't do that last night.

She moved forward like a sleepwalker, knowing that they'd already claimed her whether they knew it or not. She stepped into Kir's open arms, enjoying the feel of him as he wrapped himself around her. "Do your worst, blondie."

The snort from the shower had her grinning up at Kir, easing the strange tension that had filled her at Kir's command. She looked past Kir to see Logan washing up, his cock already hardening as he ran the washcloth over his body. "Yeah, babe. Do your worst."

"Oh, I intend to."

Jordan gasped as Kir picked her up, put her on the counter and entered her in one long, slow thrust. By the time he was fully seated she would swear she could taste him in the back of her throat.

"Love you," he whispered against her lips before taking her mouth the way he'd taken her body, slowly and thoroughly.

She kissed him back, pouring all of her love into it, trying to say without words what she knew he wanted to hear.

"Fuck!" Kir's mouth lifted from hers with a gasp, his hips stilling in mid-thrust. "Logan, warn me, damn it!"

"You didn't honestly think you two were going to have *all* the fun, did you?"

Kir frowned over his shoulder. Jordan saw Logan, really, *really* close behind Kir. Kir was quivering, his eyes closing on a sigh as Logan's hips rolled.

"Logan, are you…?"

He laughed huskily. "Hot, wet, blond sandwich. Lunchtime."

Jordan shook her head, her eyes wide. Kir moaned. He opened his eyes and she gasped; the pupils were pure white.

Logan bit down on Kir's neck and thrust inside him once, twice, as hard as he could, pounding into Kir's ass. The movement pushed Kir into her and she groaned, wrapping her legs as best she could around both men.

She put one arm around Kir's neck, the other around Logan's, and squeezed her vaginal muscles as hard as she could.

Kir's eyes nearly crossed and he choked, throwing his head back to land against Logan's shoulder. "Do that again." His voice deepened the way it had the other day, but this time instead of the instinctive fear she'd felt, tingles worked their way down her spine.

"Do what?"

"Both. Either. Fuck me, both of you."

Logan's gaze locked on her face. He blew her a kiss as flames began flickering in and out in his hair. "Our pleasure."

There wasn't much Jordan could do, pinned to the countertop the way she was, but she did her best. She pulled with her legs, tightening her muscles, loving the feel of Kir's cock fucking into her as Logan pounded into him from behind.

It was the weirdest, hottest thing she'd ever experienced. Logan's hands were on Kir's hips, fingertips digging in, pulling him back, and pushing him forward as he moved in and out, in and out…

Kir's hands were playing with her breasts, twisting and pulling at her nipples, making them burn with need. Her pussy was clutching at him all on its own now as her arousal hit new heights.

"Stroke yourself, sweetheart. Come on Kir's cock."

She nodded at Logan and leaned back, resting on one elbow. She reached down and began stroking her clit, loving the little gasps and moans Kir and Logan made as they watched her.

Logan's strokes became faster, his thrusts harder. Kir's cock was swelling inside her, his face a study of tormented ecstasy.

His eyes closed on a groan, and opened again, the inhuman whites, grays, and blues covering them completely. *A spring storm. I can see the storm in his eyes.* He grabbed hold of her hips, pulling her to him as Logan pushed at him from behind.

"Oh, fuck, babe." Logan groaned and bit down again on Kir's shoulder, his thrusts becoming erratic as he came in his lover's ass.

Kir's inhumanly beautiful eyes glowed as he gasped, "Come for me."

Jordan screamed, her whole body clenching around the cock in her pussy, her toes curling, her hands clenching.

Kir's roar of completion drowned them both out.

***

They collapsed together on the bed, too spent to do anything other than pant.

"Now do you believe me?"

She looked over Kir's heaving chest at Logan, and frowned. "About what?"

"We love you."

Kir watched with sleepy eyes as the two most stubborn people he knew stared at one another over his body. He put an arm around each of them and cuddled them against him. Neither one fought him.

He smiled, his heart turning over when their hands met on his belly and clasped.

"Yes. I believe you."

He waited, somehow knowing what was going to happen. The smile he felt Jordan hiding against his side might have been a big clue.

"*And*?" Logan drawled. He felt Logan clutch Jordan's hand a little bit tighter.

"And what?" Jordan's muffled voice was filled with laughter.

"Isn't there something you're supposed to say back?"

She lifted her head from his side with a weary sigh Kir didn't believe for a minute. "Isn't that the *woman's* line?"

Logan growled.

Kir sighed and looked at Logan. "*I* love you." Then he looked at Jordan. "And I love *you*." He smiled sweetly at Jordan. "See how easy that was?"

"You know, if I wasn't half-dead from exhaustion, I'd act all coy and ask you guys to prove it again." Her head settled on his shoulder and she yawned. "Haven't even had my caffeine yet, damn it." Kir felt her grip Logan's hand back. "Makin' me say I love you's before I've had my coffee. Pains in my ass."

Kir couldn't keep the grin off his face as he felt Logan collapse next to him in relief. "No, that would be pain in *my* ass." He leered down at her smugly. "He'll be a pain in *your* ass tonight."

He started laughing when her jaw dropped open, her gaze surreptitiously checking out Logan's flaccid cock. He was still laughing when the two of them got up and headed into the kitchen for Jordan's all-important coffee, shaking their heads at him and grinning like children.

***

Jordan stared out the window at Rittenhouse Square, her jaw hanging open. "Kir?"

Logan shook his head, smiling. Apparently, they'd made Kir very, *very* happy, and Rittenhouse Square was now blooming with the results.

Kir was looking down at the Square with a smile. "Huh. Pretty."

Logan snorted.

Jordan rolled her eyes and turned away from the window. "Any news on Grimm?"

Logan stared down at her. "No. Why?"

"Because I'm going to go insane if I don't get out of this condo."

Logan leered at her. "We have ways to keep you busy." He waggled his eyebrows.

"There are only so many times a day you can have sex."

"Sure. One o'clock, two o'clock, three o'clock, four o'clock…"

He grinned when she glared at him.

The strains of Enya's "Boadicea" drifted from the den. Kir went to the den and came back with Logan's cell phone. He handed the Bluetooth to Logan, who put it in his ear.

Jordan's eyebrows rose when she heard Logan's ringtone. "What is that?"

"Give me that." Logan answered his phone, blushing. He glared at Kir, daring him to say anything, promising retribution if he did. *I have* got *to change my ringtone.*

Kir whispered in her ear, "It's Enya."

Jordan choked. "Enya?"

Logan, smiling tightly, answered the phone. "Yo, Logan here." He stomped into the den, trying his hardest to ignore Jordan's muffled laughter.

He sat at the desk and booted the computer. He wanted to see how well the YouTube video's spell was working, and the best way to do that was to check it out online.

"It's Travis. I've got Morgan and Magnus almost detoxed. How's Jordan?"

Ours, finally. "Feeling much better."

"That's good."

Logan rolled his eyes and opened the YouTube link.

"By the way, does Jordan know she's married?"

Logan froze. How in the hell…?

Travis chuckled. "Guess not. Give the bride a kiss for me, will ya?"

"When hell freezes over." All of Jordan's present and future kisses were reserved for him and Kir.

Travis laughed. "Take care, okay? Talk to you later."

"Bye." He hung up and clicked on the YouTube video, watching closely to make sure that the spell was still in place, grumbling about nosy detectives.

***

"Hey, Logan. You want some?" Jordan held up the coffee pot and shook it.

"No thanks. I gotta run. Be back in a bit." He walked out the front door, not even looking at her.

"Huh."

"What?"

Jordan turned to Kir, putting the coffee pot back down on its burner. "Logan just left."

Kir blinked slowly. "Left?"

The disbelief in his voice worried her. "Just walked out the door."

Kir tensed. "Did he kiss you good-bye?"

"No." Jordan shook her head, worried about Kir. His pupils were white.

"What room did he come out of?"

She pointed to the den, following behind as Kir rushed into the room.

"Damn. Shit. Grimm has him."

"What?"

"Look. Thanks to Logan, you should be able to see it."

He was grabbing his car keys off the hook while she glanced at the screen. Sure enough, something glowed on the edges of her vision, something blue-white and very cold. "What the hell is that?"

He grabbed her arm and dragged her to the door, not giving her a chance to see what it was. "A spell."

"What?"

"A spell! Look, Logan was probably checking to make sure the spell on the video hadn't been tampered with. He would have left himself open. If Rina cast the spell, Logan would be vulnerable to it."

"Rina? Who's Rina?"

He dragged her to the stairs and opened the door. "Val's mom, and Grimm's mistress."

"Mistress?" Jordan pictured her wrinkled old grandfather getting it on with another wrinkled, gray-haired lady. "Ew."

He was dragging her down the steps as fast as she could go. "Don't think of it as grandpa lovin', because Grimm doesn't really look like you think he looks. Remember, he's a shapeshifter."

"Right. Oh! You mean he's hot under the wrinkles?" She thought about that as they took another corner at high speed. "Double-ew." She landed hard on the next landing, but Kir didn't stop tugging her on. "Why are we taking the stairs?"

"I'm hoping to beat the elevator to the bottom." Kir took the next corner at speed.

"From the twenty-second floor?" Jordan was only grateful he'd grabbed her *good* hand to tug her along.

It took them a few minutes to run all the way down to the first floor and out the door. Jordan's legs would probably never forgive her, but if Grimm had Logan the burn would be worth it. "Why is he vulnerable to Rina's magic?"

"Opposite elements. Rina's a frost Jotun, Logan's a heat Jotun."

"Oh." They made it to the front door in time to see Logan stepping into a silver Porsche. He turned and looked at them and mouthed a word just as the car took off down the street to the blare of horns.

"Shit! Did you catch that?"

Jordan ran back into the building, Kir right behind her. "Yes. *Jamie*."

She was dialing Travis's number as she ran.

Chapter Nine

Kir drove like a bat out of hell to Grimm's house, per Jordan's orders. He had no intention of arguing with her. From the look on her face, she had something planned. "He's not going to take Logan there."

"I know." Her voice was calm, but her hands were shaking as they pulled into the driveway. "Wait here."

Kir watched as she got out of the car, stunned. *Oh, no. Kir is done playing good doggie.* He got out and followed behind as she rang the doorbell.

A flare of red and white flashed on the edges of his vision as Jordan's magic countered Rina's. *How in the hell did Grimm convince Frigg to let his mistress ward their house?* Fire won, melting the ice-magic. *Damn, she's strong. Logan's going to have to start training her right away.* He suppressed the shiver of fear that Logan wouldn't be around to train her.

"Jordan?"

For the first time in over a millennium Kir looked in the face of his mother…and felt nothing.

"Hi, Grammy. We've got a problem." Jordan turned and looked at him, but he couldn't take his eyes off the woman who'd mistreated his brother. All because Hodr was blind, and he wasn't. She'd virtually ignored his brother, pushing him aside in favor of the "perfect" son.

Okay, the memories helped. Now, when he looked at her, he wanted to throw up.

"Baldur?" Frigg took a shaky step forward. "Is that you, Baldur?"

He frowned. "I was. A long time ago."

She looked terrified. "Ragnarrok has come?"

He shook his head. If she wanted to play games with him, she was in for a surprise. He didn't have time for this. "You know it hasn't." He stepped forward, allowing the rage in him to show in his eyes. She gasped as he grabbed her arm. "Where's Logan?"

"Kir?"

He turned to see Jordan holding a silver flask. "Grammy's tonic, lovingly made by Grimm." She opened the cap and sniffed. Wrinkling her nose, she poured the contents onto the flowerbed. "Apples."

He closed his eyes and took a deep breath. *So* some *of it wasn't her fault.* "Where is Odin taking Loki?"

She shook her head, her eyes filled with tears. "I don't know."

"Grammy?" He was surprised by the affection in Jordan's voice. "I need you to do me a favor."

"What?"

"Mistletoe. You need to get Mistletoe to promise not to hurt Kir."

"Oliver said that wasn't necessary, since Baldur…Baldur…" She sniffled.

"Kir's not dead. He's holding your arm."

Frigg looked at Kir, confused, clearly befuddled by Grimm's "tonic". "His name is Baldur."

Kir nodded, hoping…

"Baldur." Frigg's eyes cleared a little as she stared at him, measuring his features, stroking his cheek with a mother's touch. "*Baldur.*" She pulled back, breaking free of his hold on her. "You *are* alive."

He nodded again, watching as her face tightened.

"I'm going to *kill* him."

"Grimm?"

"Loki. How *dare* he keep you from me?"

Kir rolled his eyes. "Loki saved my life. Long story, no time to tell it. Where do you think Grimm would take him?"

She shrugged. "I have no clue."

It was obvious to him that she was lying. He smiled. Thunder sounded in the distance. "If you don't tell me where Grimm took Logan, you'll never be allowed to see my children. Your grandchildren."

She gasped. "Nanna is alive, too?"

He gritted his teeth. "No. Grimm murdered her. Jordan is…ours."

"Ours? What do you mean, ours?"

"Mine and Logan's."

She glared at Jordan. "You would sleep with Loki after sleeping with Baldur? How could you?"

"Because I love them both! Look, we don't have *time* for this! Grimm has Jamie!"

Frigg hissed, "*What?*"

"That was the lure he used to get Logan to go with him. He kidnapped Jamie."

"Why would Loki give a damn?"

"Because *I* give a damn." Kir could tell Jordan was getting frustrated with Frigg, and couldn't blame her. She'd probably only been exposed to the grandmother Grimm wanted her to appear to be, never the self-centered bitch everyone else knew she was. "Grammy, *please.*"

Frigg took a deep breath. "All right. For Jamie." She turned to Kir. "I want Loki out of your life."

Kir turned and walked back to the car. "When hell freezes over."

"That can be arranged."

"Grandmother."

Kir saw the sprig of mistletoe hanging from the branch of a tree, and sighed. *He grows it on his property, just in case, and she never noticed. After all this is over, I have some apple trees that need chopping down.*

He picked a sprig, and smiled. *But first, I have a little something to take care of...*

***

Grimm smiled at Fred and Adam. "What do you think, gentlemen? Will we get him to talk? Or is he a lost cause?"

"I say we kill him now and then go looking for Jordan. Who knows what the son of a bitch has done to her." Adam glared at the bruised and bleeding figure tied to the chair.

"Punish him more. Make him really hurt." Fred smiled. "Bring in the snake."

Grimm looked with approval at his oldest son, the one who'd never managed to disappoint him. "Very good! I like that." He turned to Val. "Bring the snake, Val."

Val nodded and left the room, his stride unhurried.

Grimm shook his head. If he hadn't stepped up to the plate and brought him Loki, Val would have been the one tied to the chair. Maybe he could afford to give the boy a reprieve.

"You never did explain how you managed to get Loki to come out of hiding, you know."

He looked at Fred with a smile, thinking of the girl he'd left tied, broken and bleeding, to the cross in the room off this one. "Let's just say, I finally figured out his weakness." *The traitorous bitch.* Jordan was going to find herself tied where Jamie was very shortly.

No one crossed Grimm and lived. Not his children and certainly not his grandchildren. When would they learn?

***

151

Val hurried into the room Jamie was tied in, his heart nearly stopping at the damage Grimm had inflicted. If he'd been present when Grimm had taken Jamie he would have risked everything to save her.

But he hadn't. Grimm had acted without him. *Tricky bastard.*

To save Jamie, Val had brought Loki to his father. The only thing he'd managed to salvage out of this whole fiasco was changing Grimm's message from a compulsion to just that: a message.

Being half-Jotun had its uses. *And thank you, Loki, for stepping up to the plate and once again taking punishment you don't deserve to save someone else.*

He untied Jamie, careful of her wounds, and picked her up, brought near to tears when she moaned and sucked in a deep breath. Too much longer and she would have suffocated to death, the pressure of hanging by her wrists too much for her body to bear. He cradled her gently in his arms and walked out, feeling the shiver of power in the air.

Baldur was coming. And Grimm was finally going to pay. Too bad he wouldn't be there to witness his brother being avenged.

"*Val.*"

He looked up to see Travis, horrified, staring at Jamie, and knew there was no way he could explain it. Not with the game he'd been playing for far too long. "It's a trap."

Travis's eyes were turning blind, never a good sign in the God of Justice. He felt the god's power wash over him, a cold breeze that slowly warmed inside him. "Tell me."

"Grimm. He's got Loki tied to a chair. He's torturing him. Now hurry. I have to get Jamie to a hospital."

Jamie groaned, distracting him. "Uncle Val?" She tried to open her eyes but they were too swollen and bruised.

He smiled down at her. "It's okay, pumpkin. I've got you." For however long Travis would let him live, anyway. He walked away, his shoulder blades itching the entire time, waiting for a blow that never came.

***

Logan groaned as yet another blow landed on his side.

"Where's my daughter, you piece of shit?"

He laughed, knowing how it would infuriate Fred Grimm.

He was right. Fred freaked, digging his fingers into Logan's side, right where some ribs were broken. Logan bit back a scream, laughing up in the other man's face. He'd been the belle of the ball at this dance before; they weren't getting anything out of him this time, either. He was in a ten by ten room with concrete floors, only one, tiny window way up high in the wall, and only one exit. Son of a bitches had gotten at least *one* thing right. There was no way to escape except through them. And since his one major weakness was the inability to fly in any form he took without some kind of magical assistance, he was well and truly stuck.

He glanced up at the security camera in the corner of the room. A simple twist of reality had activated it. It had been easy to do, during one of Fred's swings. They'd been so captivated with making him hurt they hadn't checked to see if he'd done anything other than laugh.

All of the Aesir and Vanir were now privy to his torture, no doubt glued to their chairs, sitting on their self-righteous asses as he got beat with Mjolnir.

"Where's that damn snake?"

Hopefully it met a really big mongoose.

Grimm looked towards the door, his expression concerned. "I don't know." He looked back at Fred and frowned. "Perhaps I'd better go check."

"No need." Travis stepped through, glowing brightly, his eyes completely white.

Yee-haw, the cavalry is here. Ow. He winced as he tried to straighten up with a pained smirk. "Hey, Lefty."

"Hey, Hothead. Ready to go?"

"Oh, hell yes," Logan chuckled painfully. "Right after you rip Grimm's testicles off. I want to stick around to see that."

He had to bite back another scream as Fred Grimm swung Mjolnir and broke his right arm.

Hell. Jordan had better stay far, far away from here. *If Kir brought her with him, I'm going to be supremely pissed off.* She did not need to see her father and stepfather torturing him.

"Your daughter is on the way to the hospital, Fred."

Oh, shit. That meant Jamie was in bad shape. He'd hoped that, by coming with Val peacefully, the sons of bitches wouldn't hurt her too badly.

Guess he'd been wrong. Yet another thing to set at their doors and make them pay for.

Travis's gaze remained locked on Grimm's, his arms loose at his sides. He was waiting for the Old Man to make a move. From the look on his face, he was *eager* for it.

"Jordan?" Fred stepped away from Logan. His expression was filled with hope and fear.

"No. Jamie." Travis smiled as Grimm's eyes narrowed. He completely ignored Fred's gasp. "Yes, Old Man. I found her. And I want to know one thing." Travis's body was suddenly glowing so brightly it hurt to look at him. "Did you rape her before you beat her and crucified her?"

Logan looked at Travis and shivered as the full blast of the God of Justice's anger swept through the room.

Grimm screamed, the power flowing through him, unable to stop the sheer magnitude that was Tyr in his justified wrath.

The shining figure of Tyr glided into the room, a glowing spear appearing in his left hand. Logan's jaw dropped when he saw it. It was *Gungnir*, the Godspear, the symbol of Odin's power.

So the rumors are true. Tyr handed Grimm the Godspear and stepped aside, letting him rule the gods. Son of a bitch. Which meant two things. Tyr was the oldest of them all. And he had the power to take back the gift he'd given Odin.

Which he'd just done.

"You may not have raped her—"

Logan sagged in relief.

"—but you tortured her. Your own grandchild. You murdered women and children, sacrificed them on the altar of your greed and lust for power. *No more*."

Grimm laughed, and it wasn't a good one. "Fred. Adam. Stop him."

Fred and Adam stood there, staring between the two men, fighting the compulsion in Grimm's voice.

"He tortured your daughter, Fred. Made Jamie bleed, and now he's blaming me for it. Do something!"

Fred blinked, and slowly began moving forward towards Tyr.

"Don't bother."

Kir. Logan's eyes closed in relief. Even with his healing, the shit they'd been doing to him had *hurt*. And now this little side-trip into Hell could come to an end.

Kir stepped in, glowing, to stand beside Tyr. Both gods were glaring at Grimm. "Hi, *Dad*. Miss me?"

Grimm's eyes narrowed. "Imposter."

Fred and Adam had stopped again, turning back and forth between the three men with dazed expressions on their faces. Logan snorted.

"Logan?"

Oh, hell no. He glared at Kir, who shrugged. "Tell me you did *not* bring Jordan here, Kir. Please, tell me you didn't."

"Oh my God. Logan, are you all right?" Jordan started to rush forward, only to be stopped by Kir.

"Don't worry." Logan grinned, knowing it was lopsided. "It's only a flesh wound." He tasted copper and licked his lips. His split lip was bleeding again.

"Untie him *right now*." Jordan growled at her fathers, her little fists clenched at her sides.

The ropes binding him came undone. He cocked an eyebrow at her. "Been practicing, have we?"

She flushed as he stood, twisting his neck to work the kinks out. "I wish, maybe I would have been able to get here sooner."

He shook his head, knowing he'd have to explain to her later the nature of their magic.

"Is Jamie all right?"

"She's on her way to the hospital as we speak," Tyr replied. Gungnir was pointed firmly at Grimm.

Jordan glared at both her fathers. "Did they know?"

Tyr shook his head. "No."

Grimm held his hands out, smiling softly. "Come on, Travis. You know me. Can you honestly picture me hurting my granddaughter?"

"Yes."

Grimm lowered his hands, his expression hurt. "How can you say that?"

Travis pulled his hand back. "Because Baldur, who is supposed to be dead, is standing right next to me. You lied to us, Grimm. You lied to us all. You used Idun's apples to keep us all under your spell."

Logan saw a familiar figure slip into the room. He wondered why no one else could see him, and tensed, getting ready to throw himself in front of Jordan and Kir, but with his injuries he might not make it in time. His arm and ribs were mending, but they throbbed, nearly blinding him with the pain.

"Once the spell of the apples wore off I saw your lies for what they were." Tyr's glow intensified. "And now you will pay."

The figure moved, and Logan leapt.

But the shadow didn't move to Kir or Jordan. It went straight for Grimm.

Grimm gurgled as Vali slit his throat. "For Jamie." He moaned as Vali pierced his heart. "For Hodr." The younger god looked straight at Kir, and pierced Grimm's femoral artery. "For Baldur."

Grimm dropped to his knees, and Vali drove the dagger into his back, severing his spinal cord. "For Loki." He watched with dispassionate eyes as Grimm collapsed, blood pooling beneath his body. He stepped back to watch his father die, his eyes cold and hard.

Then he took his dagger and attempted to pierce his own heart, only to find his wrist grasped firmly in Tyr's. "You have to let this end now, Tyr. My purpose is done."

"What purpose? To torture us?" Logan was all for the other man's commitment to suicide. Hell, he was ready to look for some popcorn. He wondered if Val would wait long enough for him to go get some from the employee break room.

"You're why Kir and Logan are still alive, aren't you?" Jordan was staring thoughtfully at Val, who refused to meet her gaze, or anyone else's. His arm strained against Tyr's hold, muscles bulging. "You kept Grimm from succeeding, but you had to make it look good." She smiled, that sweet, sweet smile Logan loved so much. "You were playing double agent, weren't you?"

Val's eyes closed, his shoulders slumping. He quit pulling against Tyr's hold. "My purpose is done, my brothers avenged. The betrayer is dead."

Everyone looked down at Grimm's body...

"Fuck. Son of a bitch. Mother fucker." Logan turned and saw the small window was open. He rubbed his eyes tiredly. "Why the hell didn't I see that one coming?"

"How did he get away?" Kir was glaring at the spot Grimm had been. His eyes followed the trail of blood across the floor, up the wall and out the window. "He could be anywhere by now!"

"He shouldn't have survived that." Logan limped over to the window, pushing Adam Grey out of his way to do so. The other man was so stunned he didn't protest. "Unless..."

"He blood-bonded with my mother, I know that. It's possible he bonded with some other Jotun until he received the power to heal." Logan and Val exchanged a look. Logan still wanted to see Val writhing on the end of a pointed stick, but he wanted to see Grimm there more.

"You pierced his heart. Unless Hel gave him a free pass, he should be dead." Jordan frowned, confused. "Shouldn't he?"

Logan frowned, thoughts racing through his mind. If Grimm had survived his wounds, wounds that would kill even a god, how *had* he gotten away? "Good question."

***

Jordan watched as all of her relatives gathered in Grimm and Son's main conference room. Logan had been cleaned up as much as possible, but she still saw red every time she looked at her fathers. For their part they couldn't quite meet her eyes, the effects of Grimm's potion still strong in their systems. Kir was keeping a close eye on them, making sure they didn't get any closer to the three of them.

Frigg was seated in Grimm's old chair, her face cold and hard as she stared at Logan. Logan ignored her, whispering to Kir as the others filed in and took their seats. Frieda Grey took a seat by her brother, her eyes wide as they went back and forth between Kir, Logan and Jordan. Morgan and Magnus sat somewhere in the middle, somehow managing to look both protective and shamefaced at the same time. It was an interesting look for her older stepbrothers. The fact that both men had come to the three of them and offered their apologies, along with a death threat should either of the two men ever make her unhappy, hadn't hurt.

"Y'know, the name thing is still kinda confusing. Frigg is Frederica, Freida is Freya, et cetera," Jordan whispered to Logan as she patted his chest. She hadn't moved from his side since they'd left the basement, worry clearly written on her face despite the fact that almost all of his wounds had healed.

He snorted. "Get used to it, sweetheart." He kissed the top of her head absently and turned back to Kir.

She rolled her eyes as a blonde woman swept into the room. Jordan didn't know who she was until she smiled sadly at Logan, ignoring Kir.

Logan nodded briskly, wrapping his arms around Jordan and pulling her tight to his chest. "Sigyn."

Her eyes widened as they flew to Jordan. "Sydney. Sydney Saeter." She held out a hand for Jordan to shake.

Jordan turned to Logan. "Saeter?"

He grimaced. "We're divorced."

"Oh." She shook Sydney's hand, not surprised when the woman's gaze traveled between the three of them, ripe with speculation. Sydney sat near Magnus and Morgan, completely ignoring Frederica.

A few other people Jordan didn't recognize wandered in. She expected they were the rest of the gods.

Frederica stood. "We are gathered here to welcome back one of our own, long thought lost to us." She gestured with a smile to Kir, her voice warm and loving. "Baldur. Welcome home."

The room erupted into polite applause. Logan rolled his eyes and leaned back in his chair, legs stretched out, and crossed his arms over his chest. From the look on his face he was expecting a good show.

Kir stood. "My name is Kiran now. Baldur died the day his father pierced Loki's heart with an arrowhead of mistletoe." He stared around the room, his expression devoid of warmth. "Anyone who calls me Baldur will be ignored." He sat back down and stared at his mother.

Jordan whistled silently at the cold rage in Frederica's eyes. "And, of course, we must elect a new head of the firm." She ignored Logan's chuckle. "I nominate Bal... Kiran, who was born to lead us, on one condition, of course."

Jordan saw Logan's fists clench. Kir's jaw tightened. "I refuse to give up my relationships with Logan or Jordan, Frigg. Get over it."

She glared at Logan. "He is the sole reason you were taken from us, kept from us, for so long."

"No. That would have been Daddy Dearest, remember?"

Val entered the room, followed by Tyr. "And I'm going to hunt him down. Hodr still needs to be avenged. But I could use some help." He stared around at the stunned faces of the other gods. Jordan was the only one who smiled at him.

No matter what else he'd done, he'd kept her men alive. She owed him.

Tyr nodded. "You have it." He ignored Val's startled expression and turned to Kir. He held out the Godspear with a grin. "This belongs to you."

Logan watched as Kir's lip curled. His long, strong fingers took the spear from Travis's hand.

Frigg's gloating expression turned Jordan's stomach. The sweet-natured Grammy she knew had turned into a self-centered shrew. She was almost tempted to ask Logan to make her some applesauce just to get her Grammy back. "Congratulations, my son. You are now in your rightful place as king of the gods."

"No."

Tyr's brows rose. "You were always meant to lead the gods. You know that."

Kir laughed. "Yes, but, you see, they never said *which* gods." He waved a hand at the men and women seated around the conference table. "As far as I'm concerned, the majority of them can rot in hell." He turned to Val, ignoring the outraged gasps of the others. "You...you I'm putting on probation, along with Magnus and Morgan."

Val gulped.

Logan growled. Jordan hid her smile behind her hand. *If Kir and I gang up on him, we should be able to win him over.*

Kir gently lifted her face. "You and Logan are going to be by my side for the rest of eternity."

"Now, blondie, we need to discuss that." Logan's arm went around her shoulder to tug her closer. "She's not immortal."

Jordan and Kir exchanged a grin. "She is now."

Logan's brows shot up. "How?"

"Mistletoe scratches."

"You mean, you two bonded?"

Kir nodded.

Logan collapsed in relief. "Thank God. I actually thought I was gonna have to ask Lefty for a favor." He shuddered.

"Get over yourself, hothead." Travis grinned. "Oh, hey, by the way, congratulations! When were you going to make the announcement?"

Jordan turned to stare, confused, at a wide-eyed Logan. *What announcement?* From the devilish gleam in Travis's eye it had to be good.

Logan was shaking his head at Travis. "Ix-nay, Lefty."

"What announcement?" Jordan was looking back and forth between the two men, her suspicions roused. They were roused even further when Kir turned his back, his shoulders shaking, tiny little snickers escaping despite his attempts to muffle them.

Travis's grin was pure mischief. "The announcement of your marriage to Logan, of course."

More outraged gasps filled the room as Logan stood. Jordan smacked Logan on the arm. "When did I get married? And why wasn't I invited?"

Jordan glared. Kir sputtered.

Logan groaned. "Gee, thanks a lot." He stared at Val. "Need any help hunting down Grimm?"

Val's lips twitched. "I think you have more important things to take care of right now." He nodded at Jordan, a soft smile on his harsh face, the uncle she'd grown up loving finally revealed to her men. "You're in good hands, honey. They'll take care of you."

She took a deep breath. She'd deal with Logan later. "How's Jamie?"

"She's hurting. I took her to Jefferson; they're taking good care of her."

"Good." She turned to ask Travis a question, but the other man was gone. "Huh."

"You ready to go?" Kir took one hand, Logan the other.

"You can't leave." Frederica stood, her glare equally divided between Logan and Jordan. "You have responsibilities."

Kir tugged at their joined hands until the three of them started moving towards the front door. "You're absolutely right, Mother." He grinned. "I think I need to pay a visit to Hell."

He laughed as he tugged his lovers out of the room.

"Hell?" Jordan stared at the back of Kir's head. She turned to look up at Logan, who was grinning. "Is he serious?"

He looked down at her. "Look on the bright side." The two men tugged her into the elevator and hit the button for the first floor. As the door closed, Logan winked at someone over her head. "You'll never be bored."

She heard a chuckle as the door closed. She wasn't very surprised when Kir hit the emergency stop button halfway between floors. The two of them were desperate to reaffirm their bond with Logan, make sure he was safe and all right. Part of her knew what they were about to do was completely insane, but if they weren't safe together, when were they safe?

When Kir started unbuttoning her blouse she stopped him. "Logan first."

They turned and grinned at him.

The heat in his gaze alone drove the temperature in the elevator up a few degrees. A bead of sweat dripped between Jordan's breasts, testament to the fact that the temperature really *had* gone up.

Logan's eyes followed the path. "Clothes off."

Kir began slowly undressing her while Logan quickly undressed himself. He joined Kir, both of them stopping to give her little nibbling kisses down her breasts, to her stomach, and down each leg. They carefully avoided her pussy, grinning when she groaned in frustration.

Before she knew it her back was on the elevator wall, her legs wrapped around Logan's waist. His cock tunneled in and out of her with quick, almost manic strokes, while Kir stripped behind them and watched with a savage expression on his face.

"Love you," she gasped against Logan's lips as he pushed her into a quick and dirty orgasm that left her dripping and wrung out. She felt Kir gently pushing her legs aside, but didn't have the strength to open her eyes. She just smiled dreamily as Logan's strokes slowed down, caressing her still quivering flesh from the inside out.

Logan gasped and tensed. "Kir?"

"A redhead sandwich." Kir leered at her over Logan's shoulder as he thrust slowly into Logan's ass. "Mm-mm."

"Oh, shit," Logan gasped, laughing, as Kir began fucking him from behind. "Why in the hell did you bring lube to rescue me?"

"Didn't you know? He's the ultimate boy scout."

Logan's strokes began to pick up speed again. "I thought that was Superman."

"Up, up and away." Kir bit down on Logan's shoulder, sucking up a mark.

Logan reached between their bodies and began fingering her clit as she began the slow climb to orgasm once more.

Logan came first, shooting inside her with a drawn out moan. She wasn't far behind him, and from the sounds of it, neither was Kir.

They collapsed onto the elevator floor, Logan and Kir gently easing her down, careful of her shoulder.

The sound of applause echoed through the loudspeakers. "I'd give them a nine point five, if I wasn't scarred for life," Val's voice said.

"Are you kidding? The elevator thing is so cliché." Travis's voice was full of laughter. "I give them an eight."

"Ew. Just...ew." Magnus's voice sounded disgusted. "I have to go home now and scrape my eyeballs out with a grapefruit spoon. For the love of humanity, put some clothes on, people. And what the hell is wrong with you? Haven't you heard of, oh, beds? Christ, I run to the monitor thinking Grimm has you and get to see Kir and

Logan's naked butts. Dumb asses. Don't you people watch horror movies?"

It was very hard to dress a man when he was laughing so hard he started crying, but somehow Jordan and Logan managed it.

Epilogue

A small spider sat, watching in the darkness as the room was cleaned of blood. The janitor knew *something* had gone down in the room, but hadn't questioned Frigg's directives, thanks to a judicious use of apple juice.

Cold bitch. The others were feeling the full force of her wrath as she took out Baldur's desertion on them.

Inside, Grimm chuckled. He knew they'd think he'd flown out the window when he'd opened it. It meant he'd had time to curl up in a little crack in the cinderblock, giving his body time to heal, completely undetected.

He had a number of things he needed to take care of. Starting with Vali, and ending with Baldur and Loki. And Tyr.

Tyr, perhaps, would be the first to die. Without him, Gungnir would revert back to Grimm. The thought that Tyr might have passed it on briefly crossed his mind, only to be dismissed. Tyr wouldn't give it away lightly, not after he'd just taken it back from Grimm.

Yes. Once Tyr is gone, time will be on my side. After all, I have all of it.

The spider sat in the crack in the wall and spun his plans...

Travis stared down at the bloodied face of the woman he'd pined over for years. He hadn't dared to touch her, not wanting to bring her grandfather's wrath down on her head.

But Grimm had hurt her anyway.

For that alone, the other god would die.

"Travis?" Her voice was broken, barely a pained whisper, but he heard it.

He heard everything she said, whether she knew it or not.

She could barely open her eyes. She looked so small and fragile in the bed, it broke his heart. She licked her lips. "Travis, is that you?"

"I'm here, Jamie." He took her hand in his and held his rage back by sheer force of will. He wanted so desperately to brush back her hair, but Fenris had seen to it long ago that he couldn't.

He could no longer blame the Wolf for what he'd done. Grimm had been manipulating all of them, even back then. He hoped Logan had succeeded in freeing his child from Grimm's chains.

His attention returned to her as she moaned. "I'm here."

And you'll never be alone again.

Look for these titles by Dana Marie Bell

The Gray Court
Dare to Believe
Noble Blood
Artistic Vision
The Hob
Siren's Song
Never More

Halle Pumas
The Wallflower
Sweet Dreams
Cat of a Different Color
Steel Beauty
Only In My Dreams

Halle Shifters
Bear Necessities
Cynful
Bear Naked
Figure of Speech
Indirect Lines

Heart's Desire
Shadow of the Wolf
Hecate's Own
The Wizard King
Warlock Unbound

*Maggie's Grove
Blood of the Maple
Throne of Oak
Of Shadows and Ash
Song of Midnight Embers

The Nephilim
*All for You
*The Fire Within
Speak Thy Name

Poconos Pack
Finding Forgiveness
Mr. Red Riding Hoode
Sorry, Charlie

*Published by Carina Press

Dana Marie Bell Books
www.danamariebell.com

Made in the USA
Lexington, KY
15 December 2019

58597235R00105